Deep Seduction
Sexy Stories Collection

VOLUME 41

10 EROTIC LESBIAN SHORT STORIES

SHALA BREECE

Publisher's Note: This is a work of fiction. Names,
characters, places, and incidents are a product of
the author's imagination. Locales and public
names are sometimes used for atmospheric
purposes. Any resemblance to actual people, living
or dead, or to businesses, companies, events,
institutions, or locales is completely coincidental.

Deep Seduction/ Shala Breece. -- 1st ed.
Xplicit Press, an imprint of TLM Media LLC

ISBN-13: 978-1-62327-572-3
ISBN-10: 1-62327-572-5
eISBN: 978-1-62327-622-5

Printed in the United States of America

CONTENTS

1	Her Moment Of Weakness	1
2	Erotic Fruit Adventures	20
3	Her Exotic Girl Toy	37
4	Seduced By A Bra	55
5	Summer Nights On Fantasy Island	71
6	Her Personal Chef	87
7	CEO For Lunch	103
8	A Mardi Gras Affair	121
9	A Day In The Life Of A Porn Star	139
10	Seducing La Maestra	155

1 HER MOMENT OF WEAKNESS

Molly gave a long sigh. It would be another lonely weekend without her husband, Ben, who was away on business. Recently, Ben always seemed to have some business affair on the weekend that would take him away from home. Molly was almost certain that he was cheating on her, maybe with his secretary or one of his colleagues. She did not know who it was, but her female instincts were almost never wrong when it came to stuff like that. She cursed under her breath, "till death do us part, my ass," remembering the vows they had taken a few years back during their elaborate wedding ceremony.

Stretching her hand over to her nightstand, she got hold of her cell phone and made a quick call. Her call did not last long and as she got out of bed, she heard the sound of Mya's cries emanating out of the small baby monitor. "Shit," she said to herself, rushing out of her room into the nursery where her six-month-old baby girl slept.

Mya was the youngest of their four children. The others were Mandy, Aaron, and Crystal, who were thirteen, ten, and seven years old, respectively. They were all at home with her this weekend, and Molly knew that she would need some assistance in caring for them.

"Oh... what's wrong baby?" she said, picking up Mya from her cradle. Molly rocked the innocent baby in her arms, singing her a lullaby while heading downstairs to the kitchen to get her milk ready.

As she prepared the bottle for her baby, the other kids came running downstairs one by one with a burst of energy. It was Saturday, and they were all very excited. It was the day they could go out to play for as long as they wanted, come home dirty and exhausted, and never hear a single complaint from the mother, Molly.

"Where's dad?" Mandy asked curiously, as they sat for breakfast. Being the oldest, she could tell when something was wrong with her mother. Molly, who'd been feeding the baby, hoisted her head unenthusiastically to meet her daughter's gaze.

"He had some business to take care of," she said in a cold emotionless voice. "He'll be back Monday night," she added in a more reassuring tone, realizing that the kids were now interested in the whereabouts of their father.

"I – I want my daddy..." Crystal whined, as

she spit out the piece of pancake she had been chewing. She had always been the closest to her father and every time he left, she threw a tantrum. This morning was no different. She was now banging her tiny fists on the table, yelling and screaming for her dad. The plates and other cutlery on the table rattled as she continued to show her frustration by hitting the table.

"STOP IT! STOP IT NOW, CRYSTAL!" Molly commanded in a loud firm voice. The little girl suddenly stopped her actions and looked deeply into her mother's eyes. She had known that what she was doing was unacceptable all along, but still she had done it.

The other kids seemed unmoved by Crystal's actions and were all busy eating and doing whatever else that they were engaged in.

A few minutes later, a loud knock on the kitchen door distracted everyone at the breakfast table. "Tina!" Aaron shouted, rushing up from his seat and running towards the kitchen door.

Tina was their babysitter, and Molly had called her in that day to help out with the children. For some time now, Molly had wanted to do some cleaning up in the attic, and although their father was away, she decided to move forward with her plans for the day.

The young woman walked in with Aaron tugging on her dress. She greeted Molly first and then went around the table, embracing the children.

"Thanks for coming on such a short notice," Molly said as Tina sat down in the empty seat beside her. "Ben's out of town, AGAIN," she continued with an irate tone of voice.

"No worries, Moll," Tina replied with a pleasant smile on her face.

Molly offered her some pancakes and orange juice, but she politely declined, saying that she was stuffed. Her sister had been having a small children's party and they had been up early in the morning baking and preparing the snacks. "I had so much cake dough I think I'll shit myself." She immediately looked around the room, realizing that the children were still around.

"Oops, sorry. Excuse my language," she apologized quickly. Thankfully, the children were not interested in their conversation and were all distracted in doing other stuff.

Molly gave her a slight smile, and they continued talking.

"I will use today to get all that junk out of the attic. It's too messy up there. I'm thinking about putting in a little gym up there," Molly informed her.

"Yeah, a gym would be great. I could work out here for free when you guys get home," Tina laughed. She had always been a little tight with her money and very cautious about her spending. The gym that she was enrolled in cost her about twenty dollars a month, and she was willing to do just about anything to get the workout without the cost.

"Sure you can work out here. Of course," Molly assured her, as she stood up from the table clearing up the plates and cups that they had just used for breakfast.

"Oh, hey, Moll," Tina called out to her just

as she was walking over to the kitchen sink. She turned back to hear what the young woman had to say. "I was just wondering whether you want me to help you with the cleaning and stuff. I've been up there, and it seems like a lot to take on in one day for one person."

Molly nodded her head in agreement; she did want the help but Tina had to take care of the kids so she had not asked.

"I could drop the kids off at my sister's place. And since she's having a party, it's like killing two birds with one stone. You get help with the cleaning and they get to go to a party," Tina laughed out loud. She felt like she's a genius; it was a brilliant idea.

"Will your sister be okay with that?" Molly asked, not sure whether she was willing to entrust her children to the care of a stranger.

"Yeah, sure. She won't have a problem with it. You can meet her when we go by there," Tina promised as she flipped her cell phone open to call her sister, Linda, to inform her of their plans.

"Great!" she said to the person on the other end of the call, then shifted her attention to Molly. "It's all set."

It took a little over an hour to get the kids ready and soon Molly pulled out of her driveway in her black Range Rover, trailing close behind Tina's blue Sedan. They were headed to Linda's house about thirty minutes away.

Soon they were outside Linda's house. A short, middle-aged woman ran out to greet them in the driveway. Molly watched as Tina jumped out of her car and walked up to her. Molly got out of the vehicle and walked around to the back seat to get Mya out of her car seat. Her other kids soon got out of the vehicle and followed their mother's lead.

"Hi, you must be Molly. I'm Linda, so nice to finally meet you." The woman stretched out her hand to greet Molly.

After they shook hands, she invited Molly and the kids inside and out of the hot sun. Molly went inside briefly and examined the environment to ensure that it was safe for her kids. Finally, Tina got up from her seat on the couch and informed her sister that they had to be on their way back to do some cleaning. Linda nodded understandingly and walked Molly and Tina to the door, saying that she would call them when the party was over. Molly thanked her profusely for assisting in babysitting her children. But Linda was very humble about it and did not want to take any gratification from Molly.

The two women left and headed back to the house to begin the long, drawn-out cleaning process.

A few minutes later, they were back home and Molly led Tina upstairs to her quaint little attic. As they opened the squeaking door, they were greeted by boxes upon boxes of stuff. The room was stuffy and filled with cobwebs. Molly walked over to the window and opened it wide, hoping that the room would get enough fresh air. Pulling down on a string above her head, she turned on the small light bulb in the room.

The two of them soon began cleaning up, unpacking each box and going through the contents, throwing away most of the older stuff that they found. Tina found a box marked "Fun." The name alone had her very curious about the contents of the box.

"What's in here, Moll?" she asked as she ripped off the clear plastic tape.

Before Molly could say a word to warn her about the items inside, she had pulled out a long black object. She gasped at first, then gave a wicked little smile. "Molly...," she said, holding the item in the air, making it clearly visible for Molly.

"What, you've never seen a dildo?" Molly mustered up some courage and said boldly.

Tina moved in closer to Molly, dragging the box behind her. One by one, she pulled out the items that had been well hidden in the "Fun" box. There were handcuffs, blindfolds, dildos, mouth gags, anal rings, vibrators, and even a strap-on penis. "A strap-on!" Tina said in disbelief, locking gazes with Molly who was now almost speechless.

She had completely forgotten about this box of sex toys that Ben had bought for them over the years. The strap-on had been for an experiment. Ben wanted her to use it while fucking one of his girlfriends in a little ménage à trois that they had planned. What a horrible idea it had been. After that threesome, her husband was never the same. Maybe he had decided to continue the ménage à trois without her.

"Wow, you guys must have really had some wild times," Tina chuckled as she searched the bottom of the box, trying to see if she had missed anything.

"Got it," she finally said, pulling out a small device that she placed onto her index finger. "Oh, snaps! It's the tickler!" she exclaimed. Her enthusiasm was very apparent to Molly, who was startled at her reaction to one of the smallest devices in the entire box of toys. "I've wanted to try this for some time now, but I could never get it when it's in stock," Tina admitted as she examined the device that she had placed on her finger.

"We can try it now," Molly blurted out, covering her mouth sheepishly soon after. She was startled at the words that came out of her mouth. Why had she said something like that? Tina could get offended and walk out without ever coming back to work again.

"Oh gosh, I am so sorry," she apologized profusely, hoping Tina would overlook the slip of her tongue.

Tina gave a warm smile that took her by surprise. "It's okay, Moll. It's nothing to be embarrassed about, trust me." With that, she moved closer to Molly, less than an inch apart from her body. They could feel each other's hot breath, and as Molly looked into her eyes, she saw nothing but raw passion and desire.

"I'd love to try it out on you," Tina teased, running her finger along the length of Molly's arm.

Molly had been wearing jeans and a tank top, while Tina had a simple white summer dress that stopped a few inches above her knees.

Right there in that moment, the two felt a hidden passion that had been suppressed between them for some time now. Tina had seen what Molly was enduring with her husband, and she had always wished to have Molly for just one day to pleasure her and to make her forget about her troubles. It seemed like the opportunity had finally presented itself.

With a swift movement, Tina captured Molly's lips in a hot wet kiss. Waves of passion coursed through Molly's entire being as a soft moan escaped her tender lips. Tina pulled away briefly, looking at Molly directly in the eye.

"You know how long I've wanted to do that?" she whispered in a husky, desire-filled voice.

"Too long," Molly replied, capturing Tina's lips with hers. They were both hot for each other, and the more they kissed, the stronger the urge to fulfill their desires became. Tina's hand soon found its way to Molly's body, stoking her flesh.

Their bodies ached for each other and soon they were ripping away each other's clothing in the heat of the moment. Once naked, Tina instructed Molly to lie on the floor; she was going to use the tickler on her.

She did not even have to ask Molly to spread her legs; Molly had done it already. Tina stroked her tights one last time before parting her already wet pussy. She pressed the small "on" button on the clit stimulator, and a soft humbling vibration sound emanated from the device. Molly looked down, giving her a little smirk, well aware that she was about to have the time of her life.

"Oh my God!" she moaned breathlessly, trying to grip onto something, anything, to help her cope with the immense pleasure that she was feeling. Tina was running the device all over her clitoris and the tiny rapid vibrations were driving her insane. She swelled hard, trying to control her breathing as Tina pleasured her with the tickler. Her body jerked viciously against the device as her passion grew. Her legs were stretched out forcefully as sensations gripped her entire body.

"Shit, fuck!" she moaned even louder as Tina increased the speed of the vibrations. She looked down at the young girl and saw the devious look that she had in her eyes. Molly felt her juices exploding out of her temple of delight as Tina continued to work the device over and around her swollen clitoris, increasing and decreasing the speed as she felt fitting. She closed her eyes and threw her head back, letting out a series of loud moans.

Suddenly she felt nothing. She opened her eyes and looked down at Tina. "Enough of that," Tina teased, pulling out another toy that she had hidden behind her back.

It was a huge, rough-looking black dildo. "You're ready for this, Moll?" she asked with smirk on her face. Tina spread the pink flesh with her fingers before placing the dildo directly at the entrance of the slit of her pussy. Up and down, she stroked Molly's moist flesh with the hard object. Tiny spasms shot through Molly's body, and she moaned and begged Tina to fuck her without hesitation.

"As you wish," Tina finally said as she shoved the dildo deep down into Molly's wetness. A loud moan escaped Molly's lips as she closed her eyes and allowed Tina to continue to penetrate her with the long device.

Molly gave out a loud moan as the device went in deeper and deeper inside her moist core. Tina pulled out the dildo and almost suddenly rammed it inside her pussy so hard that Molly was now screaming out in delirium. Over and over, she penetrated Molly's pussy with the dildo. Finally she stopped. Molly breathed a long deep sigh of relief.

Once again, Molly was caught off guard. But this time Tina did not use a vibrator or the dildo; this time she used the real deal – her tongue. Molly clenched her teeth as a wave of passion swept through her entire body. Tina's tongue went wild on her flesh, sucking and licking off the juices of wet pussy.

"Don't stop, baby," Molly moaned as Tina's tongue ravished her tender flesh. She felt something else apart from the hot tongue that seemed to be devouring her. She felt long fingers slipping in and out of her core.

"Ohm...." She moaned, bucking her pussy to Tina's tongue, which was now moving rhythmically over her clitoris while her fingers plunged in and out of her pussy. Focusing a little over her clitoris, Tina began sucking on it harder and harder while making pleasurable sounds.

"Oh my God!" Molly moaned out loud. This was unlike anything she had ever felt before. Tina was an expert at sucking pussy; she seemed to know exactly how to lick it and suck it while working his fingers deep down inside her. She was flicking her fingers in her hole while flicking her tongue over her clitoris. It seemed like a dream come true for Molly who had always liked the idea of being sucked on by a woman.

"I'm gonna cum...," she moaned as she gripped the back of Tina's head, forcing it deeper into her core. Tina flicked her tongue viciously over her clitoris, gripping Molly's hips, plunging her fingers deeper and harder inside her with more rapid movements. The attic was filled with the sound of Molly moaning while Tina sucked almost every inch of her wet cunt.

Finally, with a loud powerful moan, Molly released and reached her earth-shattering climax. Her body quivered as Tina gently caressed her clit, gradually releasing the grip that she had on her.

"My gosh, Tina," Molly said with a look that let Tina know that she was fully satisfied with everything that had gone down. "Now you get on this floor. Let me show you how grown folks get down," Molly said cockily, giving Tina a wicked little smile with her statement.

Tina did not hesitate and the two women switched positions. She looked on as Molly walked over to the box, pulling out a device. "Close your eyes, girl," Molly called out from where she stood. Tina smiled, doing exactly what she had been instructed. She waited anxiously, excited to see what Molly was doing.

"Don't look yet," Molly said, her voice being closer now. Tina could practically feel the heat of her body next to hers. "What is she doing?" Tina wondered, keeping her eyes closed tight.

"OH FUCK!" Tina shrieked as Molly gave her a hard thrust. Tina's eyes popped open, catching the devious look that Molly had on her face. Her eyes immediately found the huge strap-on that Molly had put on.

"You like that?" Molly teased.

"Uh huh, I love it," Tina replied, nodding her head at Molly. She had a hungry look in her eyes as she watched Molly adjust the buckles on the side of the strap-on.

"There," she said after making sure she had fitted it comfortably around her waist. "You ready, baby?" she said with a smile on her face.

Tina gave a simple nod as she braced herself for the huge dildo attached to the strap-on Molly was wearing.

Molly spread her legs further and elevated them up to her shoulders. Tina let out a loud moan as Molly penetrated her wet pussy with her artificial dick. Gripping her hips, Molly began to serve a series of short hard thrusts, followed by longer harder thrusts. Tina went wild as Molly moved rhythmically, penetrating her insides over and over.

Just when she was at the brink of ecstasy,

Molly pulled out of her pussy. She flipped her over, and as she lay there on her stomach, Tina felt Molly's hand deliver a hard smack to her bare bum. "You like that, don't you?" Molly teased, delivering another hard smack that echoed through the room.

Tina winced as Molly tried to penetrate her tight asshole with the dick. Realizing that she needed to provide some lubrication, Molly pulled away.

"Oh...," Tina moaned as she felt Molly's hot wet tongue make contact with her asshole. Molly flicked her tongue all over the hole, swabbing it with her salvia. It felt amazing and Tina found herself heavily aroused at the touch of Molly's tongue.

Another loud moan escaped her lips as Molly returned to her former position, thrusting her strap-on dick into her anus. In and out she went pounding Tina's tight asshole, smacking her butt cheeks with every thrust. Tina moaned louder and louder as Molly increased the momentum of her thrusts.

Finally when Molly had had enough dick action, she flipped Tina over once more. This time she worked her way between Tina's thighs. Up and up she went, her tongue lingering along the young woman's flesh. Upon reaching her destination, she carefully took hold of Tina's clit with her mouth, tugging on it gently, pulling just hard enough to make Tina moan out loud.

Then suddenly, like a hungry lion, Molly dove her tongue deep down inside Tina's wet slit, sucking onto her flesh hard. Tina closed her eyes, clenching her teeth together as Molly ravished her pussy with her tongue. With each long hard suck, tiny spasms shot through her body and she let out several loud moans of pleasure. This was amazing. Molly was turning out to be the best she had ever had. She tried to relax and just enjoy the pleasure of it all, but she could not control herself. The feel of Molly's tongue on her flesh was a little too much for her to handle.

Molly pulled away for a little while. "Where's the tickler?" she demanded with an evil little grin on her face. She was about to use the same device that Tina had used on her minutes earlier.

Tina sheepishly pointed out to her left, in the corner where the clit stimulator lay on the floor. Molly instantly picked it up, wiping it with a napkin from a roll of napkins they had found. She placed the device on her index finger and gave Tina another hard long stare.

"Now it's my turn with this little baby," she said, shifting her gaze from Tina to the device on her finger.

Tina looked on, watching every single movement that Molly made in the corner of her eyes. A loud moan slipped her lips as Molly's finger made contact with her clitoris. The vibrations from the device were driving her to the point of insanity. This must have been exactly how Molly felt when she had been pleasuring her. The sensations seemed to emanate from the top of her mind down to her clit. Her juices oozed out as Molly continued pressing the moving device firmly against her clitoris. Her legs jerked viciously as she tried hard to control herself.

"Shit!" she shrieked as Molly slid one finger into her wet cunt. Then she slipped a second finger and then a third, moving each inside her pussy, violently jerking them viciously in and out while maintaining a devious gaze on Tina.

Molly's finger left her wet pussy and was replaced by her tongue; she flicked her tongue up and down the slit of her pussy before finally penetrating the hole with her hot wild tongue. Another loud moan and Tina was now near her climax. Molly increased the momentum of her sucking, flicking her tongue deep inside Tina's pussy while keeping the clit stimulator on her clitoris. Over and over, Molly pleasured her with her tongue and vibrator. It was like a fantasy come true. Finally, with a loud moan, Tina reached her climax and exploded her juices onto Molly's waiting tongue.

It took Tina a few minutes to calm down from it all. Molly looked up at her and gave a little smile that let her know that this was just the beginning of much more to come.

As they sat up, reality slowly began to set in and Molly realized what she had just done. She had just fucked the babysitter. Usually it was the other way around; the husband is usually the one to fuck the young hot sitter. But here she was with four kids, fooling around with the babysitter. She tried to console herself; it was just a brief moment of weakness. She remembered everything that her husband was doing to her – the cheating and the constant trips away from home. She had had one brief moment of hot passionate sex. So what?

"Everyone gives into their desires at one point or the other," she thought to herself.

2 EROTIC FRUIT ADVENTURES

L iz walked through the empty hallway of the school. It was her first day of class, and her heart seemed to be thudding so much that she thought she would pass out. She had always wanted to go back to school, and she had finally gotten the opportunity to do so. This institution was supposed to be one of the best places to earn a degree in Culinary Arts. Happy to be there, she looked at the campus map that she had been given at security to locate where the kitchen lab was.

"There it is, Lab Two," she thought to herself, taking in some air before slowly opening the door.

The students were all standing behind several counters, with their while aprons and chef hats on their heads. To the front of the class, a stout mature looking woman stood well dressed in a chef uniform that consisted of a white chef coat, white and black chef's pants and a white chef hat.

"Come on in, ma'am," her voice was warm and pleasant, unlike her gruff look. She gave Liz a slight smile with her invitation. "You can join this group over here," she continued pointing to a small group of three students to her left.

"I'm sorry, I didn't know we had to wear uniforms," Liz apologized realizing that she was the only dressed in jeans and a t-shirt.

"That's okay, it's your first day," the woman said.

"I'm Ms. Howard, your lecturer for FN210 Food Production," the woman said with a smile on her face.

"I'm Liz Hudson," Liz introduced herself as she propped her small black side bag on the floor.

"Oh I'm sorry, bags aren't allowed in the lab, Liz. Place it in one of the lockers next door in the store room," Ms. Howard informed her, as she continued to go through the papers she had on her desk in front of her.

Liz quickly picked up the bag and headed out to the room next door to do as she had been instructed. In a few minutes, she was back.

The class seemed to be going fine, until they were given the pop quiz at the end of class. Liz realized that a lot of the basic stuff like the various sauces and the various kitchen apparatus that she was supposed to know, she had no idea as to what they were. Being that it was her very first culinary arts class, Ms. Howard excused her, but warned that she would need to familiarize herself with the terms.

At the end of class, Liz decided to go to her lecturer to find out whether she could get some extra tutoring to get up to speed with the rest of the class. If only she could get a few extra classes, to introduce her to the basic information, then she would be able to catch up with everyone else. "Sure, I can help you out, Liz. But it will have to be after class on a Wednesday. I'm very busy all the other days," she informed.

Liz gave her a warm smile, happy to get any extra help that she could get. "What time will be good for you?"

"We can get together around five, if that works with you," Ms. Howard said before excusing herself and heading outside of the lab.

The next few weeks went by quickly, and Liz found Ms. Howard to be a very fun and understanding individual. They would spend hours talking and laughing while she told Liz almost everything there was to know about culinary arts. Liz found out that she was divorced; her husband had left her for a younger woman. She had kept their huge four-bedroom house in the suburbs and their one hundred thousand dollar car. "I took it all," she said laughing.

Liz admired her confidence; she seemed to be such a professional haughty woman. Liz longed to be like her one day, free, single, and independent. The two of them seemed to be getting along great, and eventually, Liz found herself growing deeply and deeply attracted to Ms. Howard, or Suzie, as she had told Liz to call her. They were now calling each other and chatting on the phone, which was somewhat of an inappropriate student–teacher relationship.

Spring break soon came, and the school was closed for the week. Who would she get the extra tutoring lessons from, considering the fact that soon after spring break, exams would be upon them? Liz called Suzie frantic and worried; she just didn't feel prepared for the exams that would follow the little break from school. She needed to call Suzie to find out what to do and inform her of her lack of preparedness.

Flipping her small silver phone open, she walked over to the corner of her apartment and browsed through her phonebook looking for Suzie's number. Her fingers trembled as nervousness gripped her as she dialled her lecturer's mobile number. After about four rings, the woman picked up the phone. Liz quickly began to share her fears with the older woman, letting her know exactly why she was afraid to take the exam.

"I just don't feel I'm sufficiently ready, I've not had enough practice, nothing, and how will I ever pass this exam? Plus, I can't even see you this week because school is out," Liz stopped and tried to take a deep breath to calm her nerves.

"Don't worry, Liz," she had said in her usual warm calm tone of voice. "You can come to my home, if anything. I will be home on Sunday, you can drop by, and we'll cook something while we go over the notes for the exam."

Liz breathed a sigh of relief. For a minute, she had panicked and thought that everything she had been working so hard to achieve might have been destroyed by a single exam.

"That sounds great. Just give me the directions and I'll be there," she said to Suzie in an excited tone of voice, before ending their call.

The weekend came almost too soon, and Liz was finally driving down to Suzie's house. The road was long and winding, and there were magnificently elegant houses along the way. The smell of the fresh suburban air let her know that she was away from the hubbub of the busy Miami City. She finally saw the sign, "Welcome to Falcona Heights." Liz counted the number houses on the right side, till she got to the fourth house, which was painted blue and white just as Suzie had described.

She pulled out her cell phone dialling Suzie's number to make sure she was at the right house, before pulling into the huge drive way. The front door swung open, and Suzie came out wearing nothing but a white t-shirt and shorts. It was quite a different look for her. Liz was used to seeing her dressed professionally in her work suits. Today, she seemed even more attractive with her beautiful silky black hair let loose, free from the restriction of the ponytail that she would normally have it pinned back in.

"Come in. Wow, you're early," she said enthusiastically, leading Liz into her huge house.

Once inside, Liz's eyes perused the interior of the elegantly designed house.

"You like what you see?" Suzie asked, walking up to her with a drink in her hand. "Don't know what you like, but I figured some apple juice might be a safe choice. You drink it right?" she held out the drink to Liz.

"Thanks, it's actually my favorite juice," Liz smiled warmly, taking the drink and bringing it to her mouth for a slow seductive sip.

The older woman walked into a huge kitchen in the back. The counter was adorned with fruits and vegetables.

"I'm somewhat of a health guru," Suzie said upon realizing the startled look on Liz's face.

She had promised to do a cooking lesson with Liz, but what she did not tell her was that they would be preparing fruits and vegetables. Ever since she started gaining weight, Suzie had put herself on a strict diet that consisted mainly of fruits and vegetables. Today, she would be preparing vegetable lasagne with a side of acorn squash with cranberry stuffing and a tossed salad.

Suzie soon started prepping her ingredients as Liz watched on. She carefully explained the use of each ingredient to Liz. The teacher was doing an excellent demonstration job for her student. However, Liz could not seem to concentrate on what was going on; she seemed to be more distracted by something else. A few minutes earlier, she had noticed something interesting.

Suzie's nipples were so perky that they were showing through her t-shirt; also, she could not ignore the fact that her gorgeous long legs were exposed. In that moment, Liz had a deep desire to use her tongue and trail upwards to Suzie's inner thighs to taste her hidden treasures.

Liz found herself subconsciously licking her lips and fantasizing about the two of them, enjoying each other's bodies right there in the kitchen. Soon, Liz began acting upon her feelings, taking slow steady steps towards Suzie while maintaining a seductive gaze with her. As she closed the gap between them, their bodies met and they locked lips together. The older woman was very receptive and did not resist the urge to kiss her student back.

Although Liz was the one to initiate to whole thing, Suzie managed to turn the tables, and she became the aggressor, kissing Liz so hard that it made her body quiver. Her tongue seemed to bruise against Liz's lips as she swept through her mouth with a series of hot, wet passionate kisses.

"My gosh, you're so sweet," Suzie pulled back briefly looking Liz directly in the eye, before capturing her lips again with another deep passionate kiss. They were so horny for each other's bodies that they soon began ripping away each other's clothing.

Suzie pinned Liz up against the counter, and stepped back a second, carefully admiring the younger woman's body. Then almost suddenly, she hoisted Liz's body onto the counter, clearing away the vegetables and fruits to make space for her body.

Suzie stroked the full length of her body from her neck down to her knees all the while maintaining a steady gaze with her. The flames of passion made Suzie's desire for her increase as she caressed her body. Her tongue soon followed the trail of her fingers, and she licked Liz's flesh slowly and seductively, stopping at the core of her womanhood. Liz's pussy was moist and wet; the flesh was full and thick with a huge clitoris. Suzie could not resist the urge to push her face between her thighs and taste her sweetness.

Liz let out a soft moan as Suzie gave her moist hot flesh a slow long suck. Her tongue teased along Liz's clitoris, flicking her wicked tongue all over it. Liz let out another series of soft moans, each growing louder and louder as Suzie increased the momentum of her sucks, sucking her clitoris harder and harder. Liz bucked her pussy against her hungry mouth as she sucked her flesh feverishly, making pleasurable sounds as she went about it. Liz closed her eyes, trying hard to control her body, while moaning out in pure ecstasy.

"Now that was just the appetizer," Suzie said, pulling away from Liz's temple of delight. She gave Liz a wicked little smile as she carefully scrutinized her pussy, stroking her wetness with her index finger. Her eyes soon left Liz's body and shifted towards the counter; she seemed to be searching for something, anything long that could be used to penetrate the young woman's pussy.

"There it is," she continued, pulling out a large carrot that was well hidden amongst some lettuce.

Liz looked on curiously as her juices slowly dripped out her pussy and onto the counter top. Every inch of her body ached to be penetrated.

"I'm going to show you how you can really enjoy this carrot," Suzie teased, stroking the slit of Liz's pussy with the vegetable.

Liz's pussy was so wet that there was no need for any additional lubrication. She moaned a little as Suzie used the carrot to penetrate her inner flesh. Suzie pushed the long carrot about half way inside the pussy and pulled it out, before thrusting it inside once again. Over and over, Suzie gave her several rapid thrusts with the carrot.

"Enough of that," she muttered under her breath tossing the carrot to the side. Once again, her eyes seemed to be searching for something.

Liz looked on heavily anticipating whatever was to come. She gasped as Suzie took hold of a huge cucumber and brought it down to her pussy. The cucumber bruised against her tight pussy, as Suzie tried her hardest to penetrate her pussy with it.

"Oh gosh, it's too big," Liz squeaked closing her eyes as she gripped onto the sides of the counter for support.

"Don't worry, I'll be gentle," a warm smile

graced Suzie's face as she brought her lips downwards.

Liz moaned out loud, as Suzie captured her raw flesh with her lips, kissing and caressing her pussy, as she penetrated her slit with the cucumber she had in her hand. Suzie sucked her flesh harder and harder, changing her momentum as she went along. As she pleasured Liz with her tongue, she used the cucumber to fuck her pussy. Suzie gave her a combination of several hard thrusts mixed with shorter more rapid thrusts. Liz found herself clenching her teeth as waves of pleasure coursed through her body. Over and over, Suzie continued to penetrate her pussy with the cucumber, forcing almost the entire length of the vegetable inside her moist core.

Finally, Liz could no longer control herself; she parted her legs further and bucked her pussy against Suzie's mouth and the cucumber. With a loud moan, she submitted her climax and released.

It took her a few minutes to calm down from the experience. She opened her eyes, and before she could even say a word, Suzie's lips came crashing down upon hers. Her lips were covered with Liz's juices, and Liz kissed her harder, indulging on the taste of her pussy.

"Yum. Delicious," Liz teased licking her lips as they ended their passionate kiss. Suzie still had a hungry look in her eyes, and Liz could feel her burning urge to have her right there on the counter.

"Now I'd like to taste you," she said as she fondled with Suzie's breast. Suzie hopped onto the counter desperately waiting for Liz to pleasure her. Liz looked on with admiration, she was amazed at how full and perky Suzie's breasts were. The older woman noticed the look on Liz's face.

"Ten thousand dollars baby," she gloated bouncing her full artificially enhanced breasts in her hands. It was then Liz realized that she had had some work done on her breasts.

"A-mazing," Liz said, stroking the nipples with her fingers. Liz's lips soon followed as she kissed and sucked onto each nipple moving from the right breast to the left. Suzie threw her head back and let out a loud moan, as Liz's tongue caressed her hardened nipples. She was getting wet, and she desperately longed to feel Liz's tongue on her pussy instead. It almost seemed like Liz read her mind because her tongue soon left her nipples and trailed downwards.

Suzie leaned back and hoisted her leg up onto the counter, parting them, allowing Liz perfect access to her moist flesh. She moaned as Liz's lips made contact with her pussy, sucking the tender flesh vigorously. Suzie gave another loud moan as Liz penetrated her slit with two of her fingers. Liz flicked her fingers back and forth inside Suzie's moistness, causing the older woman to close her eyes as she pleasured her with her fingers.

"You like that?" Liz asked as she pulled her head out of the woman's inner thighs.

"Uh huh," Suzie moaned and nodded her head with her answer.

"You gonna have to do better than that Miss," Liz ordered, jerking her fingers into Suzie's pussy more viciously than before.

"Yes, Yes, Yes," Suzie moaned, clenching her teeth as Liz rammed three fingers inside her core.

"Good teacher," Liz whispered with a little smirk on her face. She was the one who seemed to be looking for a fruit or vegetable to penetrate Suzie's pussy with.

She finally found an eggplant, "There we are," she continued, giving the eggplant a long lick, swabbing it with her saliva.

Parting Suzie's legs further, she lowered her head between her thighs and took hold of her clitoris with her lips. Suzie moaned as Liz massaged her clit with her tongue flicking it over and around her G-spot, causing her to go almost insane.

"Oh God, Liz. Don't stop," Suzie moaned as she gripped the back of Liz's head, pushing it harder into her pussy. Liz obliged, sucking her pussy harder and with much more vigor. Her pussy tasted sweet, sweeter than anything she had tasted. Almost suddenly, she penetrated the slit of her pussy with the eggplant that she had in her hand.

Suzie moaned as her body tensed up. Liz took that moment to give her a series of slow succulent sucks, caressing her pussy while fucking her with the eggplant. Her juices began flowing freely, and she twisted and turned as Liz served her with a series of hard thrusts. Over and over, she penetrated the older woman's pussy with the eggplant, while sucking harder on her clitoris. Waves of pleasure shot through Suzie's body as tiny spasms rushed through her entire being. The kitchen was filled with her moans, and Liz also made several pleasurable sounds as she sucked the juicy wet pussy.

"I'm gonna cum," Suzie moaned as she bucked her pussy against Liz's mouth. With a loud moan, she reached her climax and released her juices onto Liz's waiting tongue. Liz licked all her juices, sucking her pussy so hard that Suzie shrieked. It took her awhile to calm down; as she looked Liz directly in the eye, she could see the look in Suzie's eyes, and it was one that let her know that she was fully satisfied.

This erotic cooking experience was the first in many more to come. The two women found themselves exploring each other's bodies with almost every encounter. Liz soon found herself developing a liking for Suzie's strict fruits and vegetable diet as they got closer. Soon, it was Suzie's birthday, and Liz wanted to do something extra special for her. She would cook her favorite dish, vegetable lasagne, and invite her over to her quaint little apartment for dinner.

Liz had been saving up for Suzie's birthday, and on the night, she arranged to have a limo pick up Suzie from her house.

As Suzie arrived at the apartment, there was a small birthday card hanging loosely around the doorknob.

"Happy Birthday, sweetheart. Come in," it read.

Turning the doorknob slowly, she opened

the door and walked in. Her steps were slow and precise, looking around anxiously, calling out to Liz. As she got closer and closer to the living room, she could hear the faint sound of her favorite artist singing in the background. She gasped as she saw the elegantly decorated table adorned with strawberries and bananas. Liz was sitting at the table, with one leg propped onto it. She had nothing on. Just a pair of black stilettos and a red tie hanging around her neck.

"Happy Birthday, love," she said in a slow seductive voice as her lips curled up, forming a wicked little smile.

"Wow. This looks amazing," Suzie replied looking directly at her beautiful shaved, exposed pussy. She could hardly wait to dive in, tongue first. She took slow deadly steps towards her seducer, stopping less than an inch next to her. Dropping down to her knees, Suzie found herself instinctively caressing Liz's hungry pussy with her tongue. Liz moaned out in ecstasy, closing her eyes and parting her legs further.

"Wait...Let me, it's your birthday," Liz finally managed to say. She immediately rose from her seat and led Suzie to the blankets she had laid in front of her small fireplace.

"Sit there," she commanded in a gentle tone of voice as she turned around and walked over to the table to get the wine, strawberries, and bananas.

Suzie did as she was told without hesitation. Liz was soon back with the stuff. She sat facing Suzie. She quickly poured them a glass of wine, and they made a toast to their new hot erotic relationship.

"Happy birthday, Suz, hope this night lasts forever," she smiled as she took a sip of the red wine.

The two of them conversed for a while, feeding each other the strawberries as they drunk the wine. After a while, the wine began to take effect, and Liz found herself becoming hornier and hornier to the point where she could not wait another minute without having Suzie's body.

She captured Suzie's desire-filled lips with hers, and they locked lips together in a hot, wet passionate kiss that left Liz's head spinning. She kissed her even harder and deeper as she felt Suzie's hand stroking her body. Liz pulled back briefly, raising the little black tube dress that Suzie had on, over her head, tossing it to the side when she had gotten it off her. Suzie's breasts popped out into Liz's waiting hands.

"God, I love those tits," she moaned as she took them into her mouth, sucking them feverishly. While she sucked on one nipple, her fingers fondled and caressed the other nipple. Suzie seemed to be enjoying the feeling because she let out several pleasurable moans. Liz's tongue lavished over Suzie's nipple giving it several long hard sucks. Finally, Suzie lay down on the floor, and Liz found a comfortable position between Suzie's inner thighs. With a quick pull, she ripped off the thin lace thong that Suzie had on, and tossed it to the side.

Suzie gave her a little grin as she parted her legs further, to allow Liz better access to her pussy. She too was very horny, and she soon began stroking her pussy with her fingers as Liz looked on with delight.

"Hand me that banana love," she requested with a hungry looked in her deep hazel eyes.

Liz did as she had requested and handed her the banana, waiting to see what was to come. Suzie took the fruit and swabbed it with her saliva before penetrating her pussy with it. Liz's eyes popped open, as Suzie stuck the banana all the way inside her moistness. As she pulled it out, Liz could see it lined with her juices. Liz now wanted to be the one thrusting the banana inside her wet pussy.

"Give it to me," she instructed, yanking the fruit out of Suzie's hand. "Now let me try that," she said in a husky voice. With that, she gave Suzie a hard thrust, and then another, ensuring the entire banana made its way deep into Suzie's cunt, holding it at the bare tip. Her index finger soon made contact with Suzie's clit and she began slowly massaging her clitoris. Suzie licked her lips and closed her eyes, as Liz pleasured her with the banana, and she fingered.

"Suck on this baby...It'll help," Liz reached over and shoved a strawberry into Suzie's open mouth. She had been moaning out in ecstasy, when Liz tried to stuff her mouth with the strawberry. Although it seemed like Liz had shoved the fruit almost too viciously into her mouth, Suzie did not complain; instead, she did as her younger lover requested, and as Liz penetrated her pussy, she took small bites of the sweet strawberry. It seemed like the teacher had become the student.

Liz soon increased the momentum of her thrusting and soon Suzie gave up and released. With a loud moan, she reached her climax, drenching the banana with her juices.

Liz stood up, fully satisfied that she had pleasured Suzie with just fruits. No tongue or dildo, just a banana.

3 HER EXOTIC GIRL TOY

Carmen shrieked out in pain as the officer shoved her against the wall, placing the handcuffs on firmly to her tender wrists.

"I didn't do anything! I'm innocent!" she yelled in a terrified tone of voice.

The officer ignored her, dragging her across the living room. The entire time she kept screaming and kicking.

"Let me go.... Let me go!" she continued screaming. Her screams were ignored by the woman who seemed unmoved by her actions. The officer was an older, more mature woman.

"You didn't even read me my rights, officer," she shrieked, so desperate to get out of her handcuffs.

The woman dressed in the police uniform finally stopped. Carmen had gotten her attention. She pulled Carmen in closer to her and gripped her lower jaw firmly.

"You have the right to remain silent. Bitch," she said in a slow deadly voice. With that, she ripped open the sheer white blouse that Carmen had on, causing the buttons to fling across the room in various directions.

"Now listen, you little dirty whore. I don't want to hear one more word." The officer used her black baton to give her two taps on her thighs, instructing her to part her legs.

"Not one more fucking word." This time the officer stroked her inner thighs with the baton she had in her hands.

"Yes, ma'am," Carmen replied, swallowing hard.

The officer led her to the back to a small bedroom. There she pushed Carmen onto the bed, with almost more force than was needed. With Carmen on the bed, she reached over to the side of the bed, pulling a medium-sized gift bag that seemed to have been hidden under the bed.

"Oh, what gifts do you bear, officer?" Carmen teased as she looked on curiously, wondering what was in the bag.

"Quiet, remember. Not a word," the officer instructed with a serious face.

"Wow, you're really getting into character, Renee," Carmen teased, looking at the older woman with a smile on her face.

For some time now, Carmen and her girlfriend Renee had been planning to do something fun and exciting to spice up their sex life. Bondage and sadist/masochist activity seemed like a good option, and they had finally gotten the time to buy the costumes and the sex toys that they needed for their fake police takeover erotic experience. Now that they were actually acting it out, it seemed like Renee was taking it very seriously, almost too seriously. But Carmen did not mind; it had been for a while since Renee showed such interest in anything. Ever since the accident, Renee had seemed a little distant and unhappy.

They had lost their chihuahua, Booboo, to a speeding driver who ran him over without even stopping to apologize to them. Booboo was like a baby to them. The accident had happened within a few seconds of leaving the small dog unsupervised in the front yard. Renee had been in the front washing her car when she reached inside into the back seat to look for something, forgetting that Booboo loved running around. The loud squeal from the dog had caught them both by surprise. Carmen, who had been inside, rushed out to see what had happened.

They both mourned the loss of the dog for weeks, until Carmen decided to bring home another animal. This time she brought home a small white rabbit. She was hopeful that Peter, as they called him, would not hop out of his cage and into the road. Although Carmen took a liking to Peter, her girlfriend, Renee, seemed unattached to the animal; it was as if she had loyalty to the dead dog. The accident seemed to have taken a negative toll on their relationship, and there was even a point where Carmen thought that the relationship might have been over. But now with this new idea that they had, it seemed like the spark that Renee once had in her gray eyes was back.

The feel of clamps on her nipples stopped her short in her thoughts. Carmen looked down to see that Renee had now begun her torture.

"Tonight I'm going to destroy that pussy," Renee said, giving Carmen a wicked little smile. She looked on as Renee pulled out a massive black dildo. "I'll fuck every single hole with this, baby," she threatened, kissing the vibrator softly while maintaining a steady gaze with Carmen.

The entire time, Carmen could not help but feel a little frightened; she knew all too well how Renee could get once she was really excited about something. At that moment she actually feared that her pussy would be bruised and swollen when Renee was done with her.

"Look what else I found," she continued, pulling out a mouth gag and some anal beads.

"Wow, you really went all out," Carmen teased.

"Yep. Anything for you, baby," Renee gave her a warm smile before giving her another very serious look. "Now where were we?" she asked as she pulled a whip out of the bag. Carmen winced as Renee stroked her body using the whip, giving her a series of soft whiplashes across her pussy.

"You've been a bad, bad girl," Renee scolded her. Carmen let out a squeal of pain as Rene pulled off the breast clamps before replacing them with her hot wet tongue.

Using her tongue, she traced the soreness of Carmen's nipples, causing her to now moan out of pleasure.

Renee parted her legs further, spreading

her wet pussy with her fingers, stroking the inner flesh with her tongue. At first, she gave Carmen slow succulent sucks, but after a while, her sucks became more vicious. She moved upwards to the clitoris and began sucking hard. She was sucking it with so much vigor that Carmen could hardly control her legs. Her legs jerked viciously as Renee maintained a firm grip on her hips. Renee was occasionally pulling onto the clitoris, causing Carmen to moan out in pain.

Suddenly there was a soft humming sound and Renee pulled out a huge vibrator. Carmen swallowed hard, taking a deep breath. Soon Renee had the vibrator massaging her clitoris, shockwaves gripping her entire being. Renee accelerated the speed of the vibrations and had Carmen moaning even louder and gripping the sheets as sensations coursed through her body. The huge black dildo soon followed and Renee was merciless with her thrusts; she ensured that she buried almost every inch of the dildo deep down inside Carmen's moist heat.

Over and over she thrust the dildo into Carmen's core, each thrust more vicious than the last. Carmen moaned out in agony; she was almost at the point of begging Renee to stop when Renee herself pulled back.

"Now turn around. I want to explore that ass," Renee instructed, pulling out the anal beads.

Carmen did as she had been instructed without uttering a word of resistance.

Using a pillow under her stomach, she propped up her ass so that Renee could get better access to her anus. Whatever Renee had planned would be over the top and very vicious. Carmen knew all too well that Renee could be very relentless and determined, and she laid quietly waiting for Renee. Soon Renee began probing her anus with the anal beads, putting them in one after the other. Carmen let out a series of loud moans as Renee stuffed the inside of her anus with the beads.

When she was done with the beads, she took hold of the dildo again this time and used it to penetrate Carmen's anus, giving her several hard vicious thrusts, increasing the momentum with some shorter quicker thrusts. Carmen closed her eyes and moaned out, begging Renee to stop; it all seemed a little too intense for her. But just like she had been suspecting from early on during the evening, Renee was really enjoying the experience and her pleas seemed to fall on deaf ears.

Renee finally pulled the dildo out of her anus, and soon she felt something amazing. It was hot and wet, softly stroking her anus.

Carmen looked back to see Renee's head buried deep between her ass cheeks. Renee's tongue was caressing her anus, and it felt amazing. She could feel her juices flowing freely. Renee now had the vibrator on her clitoris, stimulating her even further. Carmen knew that she was at the brink of her climax. And she began to scream out in delirium, now begging Renee to fuck her harder. In and out, Renee rammed the huge hard dildo into her anus, jerking it around viciously when it was deep down inside Carmen.

"Didn't you hear what I told you earlier? Shut the fuck up, Carmen," Renee bellowed, giving Carmen a hard smack on her ass.

The intensity of the moment was too great and Carmen ignored her warning, giving another loud moan as Renee delivered her hard smack.

"Oh you must think I'm joking, don't you?" Renee asked with a sarcastic look on her face. With that, she reached over to the bag that had been tossed to the foot of the bed, pulling it closer to her. She pulled out a mouth gag and quickly strapped it on to Carmen's mouth, instantly muffling her loud moans.

"There, much better. I don't want to hear a word from that mouth of yours," Renee ordered, giving her a little smack across her flushed cheeks.

She continued to caress Carmen's anus with her tongue, tracing the asshole with her tongue before flicking her tongue in and out of the hole while her hands kneaded the soft flesh of Carmen's ass cheeks. The entire experience felt like a great mixture of pleasure and pain. Renee had managed to inflict a certain level of pain, but she would also back it up with a series of pleasurable activities.

"Turn around, whore; I want to taste that juicy cunt now." With that, she removed the mouth gag that she had placed over Carmen's mouth.

Although she wanted to experience the feeling of total domination without any resistance, Renee also wanted to hear her lover moan and beg for more. So the mouth gag had to be removed. Carmen breathed a sigh of relief as Renee planted a soft kiss upon her lips.

"It's all fun and games, baby. Nothing too serious," Renee assured her before getting back into character.

"Now spread that FUCKING pussy, bitch; my tongue wants to fuck that sweet pussy hole of yours," Renee ordered, giving Carmen a wicked little grin.

Carmen was quite surprised that Renee's bossy attitude was turning her on; she had never seen Renee take such a dominant approach to any situation. Renee's finally getting some balls, she thought to herself, as she turned around, lying on her back with her legs spread open, waiting for Renee's tongue to pleasure her.

"Oh God, Renee...," Carmen moaned as Renee's hot hungry tongue swept through the tender moist flesh of her pussy.

Renee gave her several slow succulent sucks, licking almost every inch of her pussy. As she licked the slit of Carmen's pussy, her actions became more vivacious and she looked like a hungry lion devouring its prey.

Carmen threw her head back, moaning out, calling out Renee's name, begging for more. Renee was more than content to oblige to her wishes, and her sucks became more and more aggressive as she took hold of the dildo that had been lying next to Carmen.

"Shit!" Carmen shrieked as Renee rammed the dildo deep down into her pussy relentlessly. Her juices seemed to be squirting out, as Renee gave her several hard thrusts with the huge device. Carmen bucked her pussy on the dildo and soon she was moving in perfect timing to Renee's thrusts.

"Hold up! You're enjoying this way too much, slut. Don't you dare cum on my dildo," Renee teased in a firm voice, pulling out the dildo almost suddenly from Carmen's wet pussy. It was true: Carmen was really enjoying the moment and she could hardly control herself; her juices were drenching the vibrator.

Renee pulled back away from Carmen and took hold of her baton. Carmen looked on curiously to see what her next move would be. Suddenly, she felt the long baton forcing its way deep down into her pussy.

A loud moan escaped her lips. "Since you're enjoying this dildo so much," Renee threw the dildo to the floor and focused her attention on Carmen once more. "I will make sure you get something longer and harder in that cunt of yours," she threatened, as she penetrated Carmen's pussy with the long baton, putting it almost half way inside her pussy.

Carmen's body tensed up as she gritted her teeth. In and out the baton went, as Renee whispered obscenities to her, telling her what a nasty little slut she was being and asking her whether she wanted to fuck the baton some more.

She could hardly get her words out and she could see that the more she hesitated, the hornier Renee was getting. She seemed to be really enjoying the torture she was rendering onto Carmen. Finally, she put down the baton and caressed Carmen's pussy with her tongue. She seemed to be following a pattern of pounding Carmen's holes and afterwards caressing them, as if to make up for the pain she had been causing.

"Good girl. Calm down, baby," she pulled away briefly, stroking Carmen's pussy with her fingers as if she were trying to pat down an agitated pet.

Her tongue soon made contact with Carmen's moist tender flesh once more, but this time, she did not stop: she kept sucking the flesh, pulling and tugging on Carmen's swollen clitoris as she went along. She penetrated the slit of Carmen's pussy with three fingers, moving them viciously in and out of her wetness as she caressed her clit.

Carmen bucked her pussy against her fingers as she moved her hips in small circular motions, grinding her pussy against the feel of Renee. She could feel her impending climax approaching quickly, and she tried hard to not lose all control, but it was somewhat impossible. Renee knew exactly how to get her to let go and reach her earth-shattering climax. Renee's tongue gripped her clitoris even harder upon realizing that she was about to cum. With a series of hard sucks and long succulent licks, Renee managed to get her to explode.

A loud moan preceded her climax as Renee gripped her hips firmly, ravishing her pussy with her wicked tongue. Tiny spasms rushed through Carmen as her body quivered from the intensity of it all.

"My gosh, Renee. Damn, that was amazing," Carmen whispered as she tried desperately to get away from Renee's still very hungry mouth.

Her pussy was sore and tender and she knew that she could not take even one more lick from Renee. Backing away Renee, she tried to grab hold of her and keep her pussy against her mouth, but although weak from cumming, Carmen still found the strength to pull away.

"Now, are you ready for me, Officer Renee?" Carmen teased, rising up from the position that she had been in on the bed. The two were now ready to switch their positions, and Carmen would now play the aggressor and Renee would be her girl toy.

Carmen carefully removed the police costume that Renee had been wearing, flinging it across the room. Then without warning, she pulled down the thin G-string that Renee had on and popped her bra open, releasing her firmly rounded breasts.

Renee gave a soft slow moan, as Carmen took hold of her nipples with her teeth, biting them gently before giving them several hard sucks. Renee's body responded well to her caresses, and as her fingers made contact with Renee's inner flesh, she could feel her moistness.

"You're so wet, baby," Carmen moaned as she probed the insides of Renee's wet pussy with two of her fingers. Renee licked her lips as she continued to enjoy the teasing. For a while, Carmen was gentle with her, caressing her body with much precision.

"Now it's time for a taste of your own medicine," she whispered, pulling on Renee's nipples even harder than before. Renee moaned out as Carmen gave her several long hard sucks, pulling on her nipples harder and harder each time.

She released her nipples briefly and leaned over to their bag of sex toys. "Darn, it's not here," she muttered in frustration.

What was Carmen looking for? Renee wondered to herself, as she looked on with curious eyes. The bag had almost every possible sex toy that Renee could think of. Carmen did not say another word, but abruptly got up and left Renee, momentarily disappearing into the bathroom for a minute or two.

When she returned, she had something hidden behind her back. "Put the blindfold on, and no peeking," she instructed.

Not wanting to ruin the moment, Renee did as she was told and reached over to the bag, pulling out the black blindfold that was in it. She covered her eyes with much anticipation. She could hardly wait to see what surprise Carmen had gotten for her. As she lay on bed, Renee's heart thudded as anxiety gripped her entire being.

After a while, she felt the warmness of Carmen's body upon hers. Carmen's hand soon gave her a few taps on the leg, signaling her to open them. As she parted her legs, Renee could feel her juices trickling down the slit of her pussy; she had been so anxious that her anxiety had turned into an arousal and now she was dripping wet.

"Oh God, Carmen, hurry," she urged as her body ached to feel Carmen's touches.

"As you wish, sweetheart," Carmen teased, stroking the insides of Renee's wet pussy with her index finger.

She focused a little on Renee's clitoris, massaging it gently with her finger. Renee moaned out in ecstasy; the feeling that Carmen was bringing about was almost too much to handle. Suddenly the feeling of something else captured her attention. It was something long and hard, and it seemed to have been attached to Carmen's body. It was then that Renee released what the surprise was: Carmen had gotten a strap-on penis.

Slowly Carmen began thrusting the dick inside her wet pussy, caressing her huge melon-shaped breasts as she went along. Renee closed her eyes and lost herself in the sensations that she felt, allowing her mind to drift off as Carmen pleasured her.

Her thoughts were cut short by Carmen's husky voice, "You like that, baby? Tell me how you want it," she said with desire in her voice.

Renee used the opportunity, and as Carmen fucked her with the strap-on, she gave her clear precise instructions, telling her exactly when to increase her speed and when to fuck her harder. All the while Carmen continued teasing her nipples with her hand, pinching the nipples hard as she served with a combination of hard long thrusts mixed with shorter more rapid thrusts. Renee moaned out, begging for more and more.

"I want you to call out my name when you cum," Carmen whispered as she increased the momentum of her thrusts.

Renee liked it rough and hard and that's exactly how she intended on giving it to her. She wanted to see Renee beg for her to stop; she wanted to hear Renee's screams fill the room. In the moment, the desire to fuck Renee harder than she had ever been fucked in her life began to consume Carmen's thoughts, and so she began fucking Renee harder and harder with the strap-on dick, whispering obscenities as she went along.

Renee did not seem to mind, and she cursed at Carmen, as Carmen thrust the huge artificial dick in and out of her wet pussy. Over and over Carmen shoved the huge dick inside of Renee; soon Renee began screaming and wailing out for her to stop. But she did not.

"Good bitch, I want to pound that pussy so hard you won't be able to walk straight when I'm done," Carmen threatened as she continued to deliver several long hard thrusts.

She was ramming the dick so hard into Renee's pussy that the bed jerked viciously against the wall.

Renee was sure that their neighbors could hear them. After a while, Carmen stopped her vicious attack on Renee's cunt and pulled the dick out of the moist swollen slit. She moved downwards and captured a mouthful of Renee's wet pussy, sucking it hard, licking it from the bottom of the slit all the way to her swollen clitoris.

"Don't stop, Carmen. Suck it, baby. Just like that. Yeah, don't stop," Renee whispered as Carmen took her in and out of her mouth, sucking her clitoris harder and harder while licking away the juices of her pussy.

As she sucked Renee's pussy, Carmen could feel her own pussy drip in wetness, and she used it as motivation to suck Renee's pussy with much more passion than before. Renee bucked her pussy against her lips, and soon she was moving it uncontrollably, moaning louder than before as sensations gripped her body. Her eyes closed and her teeth clenched, she threw her head back viciously on the pillow as she moaned out even louder. Carmen could tell that she was about to come. She knew Renee's body like the back of her hand, and she could tell when Renee was really enjoying being eaten out.

With a loud thunderous moan, Renee exploded, reaching her mighty climax. Her body quivered as tiny spasms shot through her entire being. Her juices trickled out of her pussy and onto Carmen's waiting tongue.

"Good...," Carmen whispered, licking off the juices.

It took Renee a while to calm down. And when she did, she sat up and brought her lips to meet Carmen's cum-soaked lips. Taking in the bottom lip first, she kissed her passionately, licking off the cum that had been on it. Carmen's body responded and she kissed her back with such intensity that her head was spinning.

A few weeks had passed and the happy

couple were back at it again. This time they would be role-playing a different scenario. Carmen would play the role of a good teacher, while Renee would play the role of a naughty student. Carmen was dressed in a seductively professional black skirt suit, while Renee had a naughty schoolgirl costume on.

"Bring that little pussy over here," Carmen bellowed as she pulled Renee closer to her. Almost instantly, she bent her over using the long black whip she had in her hands; she rendered several whiplashes across Renee's bare ass. The skirt that Renee had been wearing was so short that in the bent-over position, her bottom had been exposed.

Carmen's tongue soon found the slit of Renee's wet pussy and she gave her a series of slow succulent licks, making pleasurable noises as she went along. She was like a child enjoying ice cream at the ice-cream parlor.

"Don't stop, baby," Renee begged as she bucked her pussy up against Carmen's mouth. Carmen's finger soon found the opening of her pussy and she stroked the moist flesh with her thumb and index finger, gently pinching and massaging her clitoris as she went along. Renee's juices flowed freely, and the more Carmen licked and sucked her pussy, the closer she came to reaching her climax. With a loud moan, she exploded her juices on Carmen's hungry tongue.

Soon after, they switched positions and Carmen found herself on the receiving end of Renee's vicious tongue. Sensations gripped her body, as Renee pleasured her over and over.

"No my little girl toy. I want you to turn around while I get Mr. Big," she teased, stepping out of the room briefly to get a huge dildo she had bought especially for tonight.

Carmen took in some air and swallowed hard, as Renee began ramming her pussy over and over with the huge device. It seemed like Renee was out to destroy her pussy tonight. With a loud moan, she exploded and her juices covered the dildo.

4 SEDUCED BY A BRA

Thoughts of my favorite ice-cream came across my mind, strawberry. Spreading her legs open even wider, I found her pinkish moist flesh and licked it like it was dessert. She moaned out, as I gave her several slow seductive licks. She tasted so good, I could hardly believe that I had this sweetness within my grasp all these years but had never even thought about sampling it. My heart thudded as I gave her a series of slow lingered licks, from the beginning of her anus, working my way up to her beautiful clitoris.

I gripped onto her clitoris and sucked it hard. Her body tensed up as she twisted and turned trying hard to get out of my grip. I ignored her movements and continued to suck hard using my tongue to make small circular motions over and around her clit. Soon her panting increased as she bucked her wet pussy against my hungry mouth. Like a lion in the jungle, I devoured her sweet pussy.

"Oh god Mel, don't stop," she moaned breathless. She was trying to catch her breath while savoring in the ecstasy of the moment. Her fingers dug into the sheets as she closed her eyes and allowed the sensations to whisk her away. With a loud moan, she summited her climax and exploded her sweet juices onto my tongue.

I rolled over, tired and spent. In the corner of my eyes, I could see that she had the same surprised look that I had. How did this happen? How did we find ourselves in such a compromising situation? I looked over to the corner of the room, and there, I saw the answer to my questions, crumbled up against the wall. Apparently, we had tossed the article of clothing across the room, in the heat of the moment. Turning my attention back to Aña, I once again felt the lust and infatuation that I had felt moments earlier upon seeing her full melon shaped breasts.

"I must confess you have the most amazingly beautiful breasts I've ever seen," I whispered to her.

Her eyes lit up as she took in her bottom lip, biting it gently before uttering her reply. "You want to taste them some more?" she teased, leaning over with one full breast in her hand. Although exhausted, I could not refuse such a tempting offer.

I closed my eyes and took a mouthful of her full breast, sucking it long and hard, while kneading the other free breast with the palm of my hand. Ana moaned out, as I worked up another arousal in us both. Soon she had rolled me over and had mounted me, kissing my lips hard, her tongue exploring the insides of my mouth feverishly with more passion than I had felt in a long time.

Her body was hot and warm, and it moved against me as she continued kissing me with her desire filled lips. My body quivered as I tried hard to control myself. The feel of her hand on my bare nipples sent shock waves through my entire being. Using her thumb and index finger, she gently pinched my nipples, pulling them a little with her grasp.

Ana broke away from my kiss and soon I was moaning out, as her lips captured my perky nipples. Her tongue felt unlike anything I had felt before, she seemed to know exactly what she was doing. Flicking her tongue back and forth on the nipple before taking it between her teeth, she gave it a soft gentle bite. The more she caressed and teased my nipples the more aroused I became. I wanted to not only feel her tongue on my nipples, I wanted to feel them licking and sucking every inch of my now wet pussy.

She must have read my mind, because her tongue left my nipples abruptly and she trailed downwards to my navel first teasing it a little, planting a series of soft gentle kisses against my flesh, before continuing on her downward journey.

Using her hands, she parted my thighs, and her tongue made contact with my flesh as she trailed upwards giving me a long slow seductive lick. Up and up she went until she got to my temple of delight.

Another moan escaped my lips as she gave

the inner flesh of my pussy a soft gentle lick. She worked her way from the slit of my pussy all the way up to my swollen clitoris. It felt amazing, and I could feel tiny spasms rushing through my body as I closed my eyes and tried hard to control myself. I did not want to come just yet, I wanted to enjoy every minute of her foreplay.

"Now here's what I want you to do for me. I want you to bring your legs up and spread that fucking pussy with your fingers. Okay?" she gave me a wicked little look as she made her request.

I did not refuse. I happily obliged to her request, hoisting my legs upwards while using my two index fingers one of each side of pussy, pulling the flesh apart, revealing the pink tender flesh that surrounded my pussy hole.

Her eyes popped open when I parted my pussy lips for her, and I could see the hungry look in them take over her entire being.

"B-E-A-UTIFUL," she whispered with much emphasis on the first part of the word, the way she normally did when she was really impressed with something.

"Now, don't move. I want you to close your eyes and enjoy, as I indulge on this beautiful cunt of yours," she said and without hesitation, she brought her tongue down to meet my pussy lips.

"OH GOD!" I moaned breathlessly, as she gave me a long lick. She gave me a series of soft long licks, sucking in all my juices. I took in deep breaths as tiny sensations gripped my entire body. I could tell she was really enjoying it, because she soon increased the momentum of the licks and was now licking my pussy with much more vigor than before. I continued to spread my pussy apart for her, allowing her better access to my sweetness. She sucked it without reservation, whipping her tongue over and around the inner flesh of my wetness. After a while, she moved upwards to my clitoris sucking it feverishly, pulling and tugging on it, then massaging it gently with her tongue.

I was enjoying it all, but I wanted more. Her actions were getting me more and more aroused and I finally got to the point where I desperately needed to feel my pussy being penetrated with something, anything, fingers, and her tongue, at this point anything would work. Our bodies seemed to be unison and soon her tongue came plunging down into the slit of my pussy.

"Oh…" I moaned as she stuck her tongue in and out of my cunt. Her tongue was hot and full of life, and she flicked it in an out of my hole, causing me to instinctively want her to remain in that position. My hand locked her head deep into my pussy, forcing her to flick her tongue deep into my hole.

When her tongue left my pussy, her fingers followed first two of them, then another two. With four fingers in my cunt, she gave me several quick hard thrusts, causing me to scream out in the delirium of the moment. She was merciless, and her voice was deep and husky, almost like a man's voice as she questioned me, asking me whether I was enjoying myself, and whether I wanted her to go harder and deeper into my cunt. This was the first time that I saw my roommate Ana really enjoying something.

She was somewhat of a nerd and when she was not studying, she was exercising. She was always a little insecure about her weight and recently she started a new exciting diet mixed with an aerobic routine that seemed to be showing good results. Could this be the cause of her sudden boldness? She was definitely more assertive, and her self-confidence seemed to have been boosted. Whatever her reasons were, I was happy she was taking this new positive step with her life. I would now definitely not want to exchange my rooms. The past few weeks, I had been thinking of changing rooms and moving in with my best friend Lisa, but now, with what was going on with my roommate, her change of attitude, and this new discovery that she was into me, I was not going anywhere. Hiller Hall room 120 was where I was going to remain.

My thoughts were cut short by the feeling of Ana's tongue residing once again on my clitoris. This time, she teased my g-spot with her tongue, while she fucked my pussy hole with her four fingers.

"Oh... you're going to make me cum Ana," I moaned, closing my eyes as my juices made their way down from the center of my spine and into my wet pussy.

It had been a good while since I experienced such fun, such pleasure, such ecstasy. I closed my eyes tightly and surrendered my pussy to Ana. It was hers to do whatever she desired. She could sense my sweet surrender because her tongue swept through my pussy with more life. She was sucking it more feverishly, licking almost every inch of my moist core, making pleasurable sounds as she went along. Her fingers were now being shoved into my pussy with much more force.

I bucked my pussy against her lips as she rammed her fingers inside my slit, causing me to moan out even louder than before. I threw my head back into the pillow as my fingers dug into the sheets.

"I- I … Am coming…" I moaned out as my legs jerked forward viciously as the sensations of my climax gripped my body.

Ana did not pull away; instead, she held firmly onto the top of my hip and pulled my pussy harder into her mouth, sucking out all my juices. Over and over her tongue licked my wet slit, taking in almost every drop of my cum.

It took me a minute to finally calm down from my earth-shattering climax. I could see the look in her eyes, a devious one; she was satisfied and content with herself. She had made me cum not once, but twice, in one night. I would have loved to get back up and give her a series of good hard sucks but I was too exhausted to even move a muscle.

"How was it? Did you enjoy yourself?" she asked, her lips curling up into a wicked little smile as a mean smirk swept across her round face.

"It was amazing," I whispered, gazing into her deep gray eyes.

"Good, I really enjoyed it too," she gave me a warm smile before getting out of bed. I looked on with glutinous eyes as her naked body strode across the room. She finally stopped when she got to the corner of the room and picked up the article of clothing that I had been looking at earlier on during the evening; a dangerous red lace bra that fully accentuated the shape of her amazingly gorgeous breasts. At the beginning of the evening, I had walked into the room after a night out with my best friend Lisa and her boyfriend, and as I looked over to Ana's side of our small dormitory room, I noticed that she was doing an aerobic routine in front of her television. A man's voice was shouting out the instructions.

I was shocked to see Ana doing the various exercise routines, wearing her gym shorts and a beautiful lace bra. Her breasts bounced up and down as she did various exercise activities. Her body glistened with the sweat and in the moment, I felt a deep yearning to be with her in more than one way.

It was then that I had walked over to her side of the room, taking slow deadly steps, stopping inches away from her hot sweaty body. She spoke breathlessly, trying to catch her breath, explaining exactly what each step was meant to do for her body. Unbeknownst to her, I had no interest in her moves; I was solely interested in removing the bra that she had on, and tasting her succulent looking boobs. She spoke for a while before noticing where my eyes seemed to have lingered a little too much, the crevice of her cleavage.

"Stop staring at my boobs, you're making me feel funny," she had finally admitted.

But I did not care, I liked what I saw and I had every intention of taking things to the next level with her. This had been the second time that I had walked into the room, to find her half-naked in that red bra.

The first time was a few weeks ago after coming back from band practice. Apparently, she and her friends had spent the day shopping and she had just got back to her room. Her bed was lined with a variety of clothes, all of which still had their price tags on them. She had spent almost all evening trying top after top, dress after dress. Finally, she called out to me, from my bed where I had gone to lay down.

Band practice had been exhausting, the bandleader and I had had a huge argument and I was not sure whether he would try to suspend me. If I were to be suspended, there was a great possibility that I would lose my scholarship. And what would I do then? My mom worked two jobs just to send me and my two brothers to college, and now just when I had seemed to land a good opportunity in the form of a full scholarship, here Mr. Hitchens on was trying to mess things up for me. In essence, my day had been one of the worst days I'd had in a long time.

I sucked my teeth softly, angry at the fact my roommate Ana, was disturbing the little peace and quiet time that I now had. What does she want now? I had thought to myself, as I slowly got out of my comfortable bed and headed to the back of the room where her bed was.

I had been caught off guard by two gorgeous melon shaped breasts halfway hidden behind a beautiful red lace bra.

Wow, I had thought to myself, as I carefully secretly admired her breasts. I had never seen such full perky breasts on anyone before, except on TV and in the magazines. I knew that her family was wealthy but I always questioned the fact, because here she had been in a cheap dorm room at an average state college. I always figured that if she really did have all the money that people said she had, she would be at another college, with her own private dorm room.

"I know you like them, but you don't have to stare so much," she teased upon realizing that my eyes seemed to have been glued onto her breasts.

"They look amazing," I admitted walking closer to her examining it inch by inch.

"I know, I got them last month when I turned twenty –two," she confessed with a little smirk on her face. "And they say money can't buy everything," she continued laughing out loud, while fondling her huge breasts through her bra.

I had to admit that I admired her cocky attitude, she had always been a shy timid person, but I did notice the sudden change in her attitude recently. I had not been sure what was causing her new attitude. Maybe she had got a new boyfriend, or maybe it was because her weight loss measures seemed to be working, I had said to myself.

"You can touch them if you want," she had said, pushing her chest forward, allowing me the opportunity to touch her artificially enhanced boobs. I touched them without hesitation, massaging and kneading them, one by one.

"Whoa, that's crazy," I teased. We used the word "crazy" as a synonym for awesome or amazing. It was just part of our college jargon.

She laughed as she walked back to her bed, picking up a beautiful white blouse that she had bought. One by one she had tried on the items that she bought, flaunting her beautiful breasts in my face, while I stood there complimenting her on how good they each looked on her. In a way, I could tell that she seemed to be getting some self-gratification out of the whole thing. Everything that she bought fit her well and she knew it deep down inside.

I could not determine whether what she did had been a ploy to get me to see her new boobs, or whether she was trying to seduce me, trying to get me to make a move and come on to her. I knew she was into women, in fact, I had heard the rumors on campus, the rumors of her and one of her female classmates making out in the back of the gym. I had even heard that she went both ways, she was into both men and women. Although I had never seen her with a boyfriend or a girlfriend, I could tell that the rumors were true at that moment, based on the look that she was giving me. It was a look of lust and desire, she did not say it directly to me, but her eyes sold her out. She was a little too flirty with me for a straight girl. That day I simply observed and read her body language. It would not be the day for me to make my move, but I was not frightened, I knew the day would come soon enough.

A few weeks went by and our relationship seemed to grow. It had changed from a simple platonic relationship to a full-blown romantic relationship. I was in love with my roommate Ana. She had turned out to be such a pleasant and loving person; I could not help but fall deeply in love with her. Besides, she had a beautiful body, and I was very attracted to her gorgeous physique. Her personality was also great, we would be able to chat for hours, and we connected on several much deeper levels. With us, it was more than great sex.

As I walked down the hallway, I had my head bent, watching the floor, carefully predicating my next step. I was headed to my room, Ana was supposed to be out of town for the weekend, and I knew it would be a lonely quiet weekend without my new lover and best friend. Normally at the end of every month, she would take a trip back home to Chicago to be with her parents. Her mom was very ill, she was on chemotherapy and her cancer seemed to be getting worse by the day. This had taken a negative toll on Ana, and she was usually deeply saddened whenever she returned back to school after spending the weekend with her mother.

Today had been another one of those days. A horribly exhausting day, I was not sure how much more of the band I could tolerate; between band practice, live performances, and tours, I hardly had any time to myself. And besides the lack of time, the bandleader seemed to be out to get me. Every day he would have an issue to pick out with me, and when he could not find a reason to argue with me, he would just make us practice a few extra hours, he knew that always pissed me off and he was sure to get a negative reaction out of me when he did that. Today had been no different; band practice had run long almost three hours extra. I was tired and spent, and I had politely let him know that I had some stuff to do so I would not be able to spend the extra time in practice.

Normally I would be in my room on the weekends when Ana left and we would say our goodbyes with a long wet kiss before she headed out the door. But today, I would be sure to miss her, because of the lengthy practice.

"Ms. Anderson, you have a choice, you can stay and practice with the band, like everyone else is doing and stop moping about it, or you can take your trumpet and leave, and don't come back. Lots of other trumpet players out there who want to join the band and take your spot. So if there's somewhere else you need to be then go, but know this, the minute you walk out of the door you will be replaced," the bandleader had threatened.

Just remembering what he had said made

me angry; so angry that my blood boiled. Had it not been for the scholarship and my mom's present financial situation, I would have quit the band altogether.

I finally made it to my room and slowly opened the door. I knew Ana had left; it was two hours since her scheduled departure time. I was sure that I would be alone in that room tonight desperately missing Ana, especially because I did not make it back in time to wish her a safe flight.

"Hey, you," the voice from my bed called out.

I gasped in shocked using my hands to cover my mouth that had suddenly dropped open. There Ana lay in my bed, wearing that same red lace bra.

"H-h... how?" I asked in shock. "I thought you had already left," I finally managed to say.

"Well I decided I would wait for you, I rescheduled my flight for tomorrow. I think it's time you met my mom," she said with a warm smile on her face.

I smiled back at her. "That would be nice," I replied.

Although I did not know how I would get to Chicago, considering the fact that I had no money to pay for the ticket, I was not very worried. My main concern was that I would finally meet the mother of the girl that I had grown to love over time.

My eyes carefully scanned her alluring body, taking in the beauty of her breasts that seemed to be begging me to suck them. I could practically hear them calling out, "Suck us, suck us, suck us Mel, suck us now."

I moved in closer to Ana, and massaged her round breasts through the bra, she moaned out from the sensations I was bringing about with my caresses. With a quick movement, I popped the bra open and her full breasts were fully exposed. My lips captured them, sucking them succulently. Ana moaned out in ecstasy, throwing her head back into the pillow as I fondled and caressed her breasts one at a time.

When I was done teasing her breasts, I moved downwards to the thin red lace thong that she had on. I gripped it firmly between my teeth and tugged onto it for a few minutes, finally ripping it off her with my teeth. She gave a soft giggle as I took hold of her pussy with my tongue, licking and sucking almost every inch until she reached an amazing climax that left her body quivering.

"Now my turn," she said with a devious look in her eyes, as she instructed me to lie on the bed in the position that she had been in. Her tongue was hot and wet, and she caressed every inch of my body. I closed my eyes and threw my head back into the pillow, allowing her to pleasure me like never before.

I came over three times; each time my orgasm was more earth shattering than the last. Finally, we were done pleasuring each other. All the stresses that I had been having seemed to be swept away under a mat. I was happy to have been seduced by a bra, because in that I had found a lover and a best friend.

5 SUMMER NIGHTS ON FANTASY ISLAND

"**L**adies and gentlemen, the pilot has now turned the seat belt sign on, please return to your seats and fasten your seatbelts," the flight attendant said in a polite yet automated tone of voice. Jen and Karla both adjusted themselves in their seats ensuring that they did exactly what they had been instructed to do by a young flight attendant.

The young woman was dressed in a royal blue uniform with the logo of the airline in the top right hand corner. She too found her seat at the front of the plane and got strapped in as the plane shook for a bit, before beginning its downward journey. They were about to land on the beautiful island of Samir.

Karla swallowed hard as the plane shook viciously from the turbulence; soon she felt a huge bump as the plane touched ground.

"Welcome to the beautiful island of Samir, where it's always sunny. Those of you visiting here for the first time, we hope you have a wonderful stay on this beautiful tropical island. And to those of you returning, welcome home," with that the woman put down her microphone and proceeded to begin unlocking the mechanical lock of the plane door.

The two friends disembarked from the small plane and walked over to the airport receiving area to collect their bags.

"Finally. Samir," Jen inhaled deeply taking a deep breath of the tropical island breeze. Located a few miles off the coast of Florida was Samir, a small tropical island with a population of a few thousand people, one of which was Linda Anderson, Jen's mother.

Linda worked as a marine biologist on the small island and her daughter would often spend part of her summer vacation with her and the rest of her vacation with her father, Andrew, in New York. Andrew was quite the opposite of Linda who had been a workaholic following her job to various countries around the world. He spent most of his days at his huge New York condo, relaxing and enjoying the returns on his investments and his retirement money. His daughter Jen was not alone; she was accompanied by her best friend Karla, who had always dreamed of taking a tropical vacation. This would be Karla's first time visiting the island; in fact, it would be her first time out of Miami and she was overly excited.

"This place looks amazing," Karla said as her eyes perused her environment, taking in the beautiful scenery.

"I know, right? I always enjoy coming out here to meet mom," Jen said, giving her friend a faint smile.

"And now that you're here, I'm going to have so much MORE fun," she nudged Jen, giving her a little wink with her statement.

The two of them had been best friends since their freshman year of college. Now that they were seniors, their friendship had grown and transformed over the years. She had been with Karla through thick and thin, and this year when her mom had died, Jen had made a promise that she would always remain close to her, to provide a shoulder to lean on.

Karla looked over at her friend, who seemed to be content to be back to one of her favorite places in the world. She genuinely felt a strong connection to Jen, and the feelings that she felt for her was so much deeper than that of just a platonic friendship.

It would be the best summer of her life, and she could tell. Jen and she had planned to spend most of their time together visiting and stay with each other's families. They were kicking off their summer vacation here in Samir for two weeks before going over to New York. The refreshing smell of the ocean seemed to linger in the air. Karla looked to her back, noticing the ocean in the background less than a mile away from the airport.

Looking over at Jen, she could see the look in her eyes, the look of excitement. "I love this place," Jen said, looking around the area with a smile on her round face. The two friends walked over to the front of the airport, where

Jen's mom Linda waited with open arms.

The drive to Linda's home was a long one; she lived on the south of the island, along the coastline. Before the front of the house was the gorgeous blue ocean, while the back of the house was surrounded by beautiful palm trees. Karla stood in awe as she looked at the area in which the house was located. This would be perfect for all the island adventures that the two of them had planned. Hopefully she would be able to go out to the beach for a swim, and go hiking later on in the evening she thought to herself.

Jen led her upstairs to a nicely decorated room. She would be sleeping in the same room as her best friend.

As Linda slept in her bed, the two young women got out of their bed and snuck out of the house. They were headed down to the beach to experience the feeling of the cool tropical breeze at evening time.

The beach was dark and lonely and the only sound that could be heard was the sound of waves crashing upon the rocks that were scattered on the shore of the sea.

"Thanks for inviting me here, Jen," Karla said, giving her friend a warm hug. The two held onto each other for a minute too long because they soon locked lips in a deep passionate kiss that left them both in a trance.

Jen's lips were soft and moist and Karla

could not resist the urge to kiss her again, this time was more intense than before, they were practically about to devour each other. One by one articles of clothing fell to the sand, first Jen's tube dress, then Karla's tank top followed by her shorts, and then finally their undies. The two young women were soon completely naked as their bodies ached for each other.

"I'm really happy you decided to join me," Jen confessed as she pulled away, sitting on the sand and inviting Karla to join her.

The two of them lay naked on the sand staring at the beautiful starlit sky. The moon was bright, and the ocean gleamed like a sea of crystals as the stars and the moon reflected upon its surface. The ambience was a romantic one and although they were both trying to keep their desires under control, they could not resist each other for long.

"I'm sorry, I cannot do this anymore, Jen," Karla finally admitted, sitting upwards and turning to face Jen, who was still lying down on the sand relaxing. They had made a promise that they would take things slow, especially due to the fact that her mother knew nothing about her romantic relationship with her best friend. It had been a few months since the two friends discovered that they were physically attracted to each other. They had consummated their love on Valentine's night in a beautifully decorated room.

Before traveling to Samir, Jen had requested that they just enjoy the island and its scenery without any public displays of affection. But tonight as they lay on the sand naked, Karla could not resist the urge. She needed to have Jen right there on the sand.

Surprisingly Jen did not protest, she sat up and captured Karla's lips with her own hungry lips. She too was so horny that she could not keep to her abstinence promise.

Karla broke off the kiss, worried that Jen's mom might see them from her bedroom window.

"What about your mom, Jen? What if she sees us?" she asked with a worried look on her face.

Jen did not seem to care; she was too aroused to think about anything else but Karla.

"I don't care, I want you now," she moaned, breathless. Jen gripped firmly onto the back of Karla's head, pulling her in closer and locking lips with her once more.

"Oh God Jen, I want you so bad," Karla moaned, kissing her even harder.

They were like two animals in the jungle, their bodies hot and wild for each other. This time, as they kissed, neither of them pulled away; instead, they moaned and panted as they explored each other's mouths with their desire-filled tongues. Sensations gripped their bodies as their tongues danced together in the ecstasy of the moment.

Soon Karla was lying in the sand with Jen on top her kissing her feverishly. Jen's tongue soon left Karla's mouth and lingered upon the nape of her neck. She sucked on Karla's flesh so hard that a small red spot was left on her neck.

"Suck my tits Jen," Karla moaned

breathlessly, heaving her chest upwards and pushing her full melon shaped breast against Jen's bare flesh.

Jen did not resist. She closed her eyes and indulged upon Karla's perky nipples, sucking them lightly at first but then sucking them harder and harder as she went along. Her hands stroked Karla's naked flesh, first stroking her thighs and then stroking her inner thighs.

"Oh yeah, just how I like it," Karla moaned out in delirium as Jen pleasured her by sucking her nipples and caressing her lean body. Jen spent a while just sucking her nipples, one at a time, from the right to the left, before finally continuing her downward journey. Her tongue lingered on Karla's flesh, moving her from her stomach all the way down to her wet pussy.

"Oh Shit!" Karla moaned breathless, licking her lips as Jen took hold of her clitoris and began massaging it gently with her tongue. Her juices coursed through her body, as the feeling of Jen's tongue engulfed her entire pussy. Tiny spasms rushed through her and she moaned out, begging Jen to suck her harder. Using her finger, Jen parted her pussy lips and continued licking her pussy, up and down, thrusting her tongue in and out of her tender slit. The night air was filled with the sound of Karla moaning out in pleasure.

"Tell me how you like it baby," Jen whispered, pulling her tongue out of Karla's hungry pussy for a brief moment.

"Lick it harder baby," Karla begged, as her hand gripped firmly into Jen's hair, forcing her face deeper into her moist heat.

"Harder!" she shrieked, as she jerked her legs viciously. She was on the brink of her climax and Jen knew it.

Jen decided to increase her pleasure by using her fingers to fuck her pussy. She thrust her index finger in and out of Karla's wetness, moving it rapidly and forcing her to buck her pussy against her hand.

"Oh god baby," Karla moaned out, taking sharp deep breaths, her body heaving up and down in the sand.

Jen increased her pleasure by adding another finger inside her, and then a third. With three fingers curled up together, she delivered several mighty thrusts, each one more powerful than the last. Karla found herself screaming out, begging for more and more. She was hungry, desperate to release.

Another loud moan escaped her lips, as Jen focused all her attention on her swollen clitoris, licking it much more feverishly than before, tugging on it, and pulling it hard. Karla could see the beautiful sky from where she lay, and as Jen pleasured her, the stars and sky, mixed with the sound of the ocean made the moment seem like heaven. The night was filled with the sound of her moaning out in ecstasy.

Jen pulled her tongue from her pussy, and locked gazes with her. She soon began whispering obscenities to her, as she rammed her three fingers viciously into her pussy over and over. Karla bit her lips and moved her pussy against Jen's hand in perfect timing. Her juices literally oozed out of her wet pussy.

Shockwaves ran through her entire being as she reached her amazing earth-shattering climax. With a loud outstretched moan she released and her cum exploded onto Jen's wicked tongue.

Making a loud succulent sound Jen licked and sucked up all her juices. Soon the two of them switched positions and it was Karla's turn to suck Jen's juices out of her. Karla took her time, teasing her nipples first before moving downwards to her already wet pussy. Jen held on to the back of her head, instructing her as she went along, requesting that she suck her pussy slower, harder, faster.

Karla did exactly as she was instructed and Jen was soon moaning out in ecstasy. With a loud moan, Jen reached her climax. The two of them lay in the sand tired and spent from it all. They were both unaware that this was only the beginning of many more fun pleasurable summer nights to come.

"So what now?" Karla asked with a devious little look in her eyes.

"Skinny dipping baby!" Jen replied with much excitement in her voice. They quickly got up and ran into the cool water. They spent almost the entire night soaking in the seawater teasing and playing with each other, occasionally sucking each other's breasts, while fingering each other's pussies, all the while enjoying the sea bath.

They finally got out of the water and headed back to the house, tired and exhausted from all of their playing. They had to creep back into the house, since Jen's mom was unaware that they had gone out in the first place.

Morning came almost too fast and the two of them headed out for a day in the sun, filled with shopping and sightseeing. Jen took Karla to all her favorite places on the island. Being that the island itself was small, it only took them one day to travel from the north to the south.

"Wow, it's like a jungle over here," Karla said, stepping into the bushes following Jen's lead. They had just got back from shopping and were now going on a hike in a small-forested area a short distance away from the house where they were staying.

"Don't worry, I got you baby," Jen assured her, turning behind to give her a hand.

Although it had not rained that day, the soil was still very much humid and soggy. Maybe it was because of the tall trees that seemed to cascade the earth, their huge branches and spread out leaves blocked off much of the sunlight that was needed to help dry of the moisture from the soil.

"Damn," Karla muttered, trying to wipe off her shoes on a pile of leaves to her side. She had just happened to step in a little mud puddle and had gotten some mud on her white tennis shoes. Thinking about it now, she cursed herself under her breath. How foolish she had been to dress all in white for a nature hike in the forest.

They continued their trail until they got to the top of a small mountain that overlooked the valley and also provided a picturesque view of the deep blue ocean.

"Amazing, it looks like we're in the movies. I've only seen such great views on TV and in movies," Karla admitted, pulling out her binoculars to get a closer look

"Take it all in baby while you can," Jen teased moving in behind her, and holding her from the back. She planted a soft kiss on the nape of her neck, as she wrapped her hand around Karla's narrow waist.

Once again, Karla thanked her for inviting her. "Ever since mom died, I've been so sad, so …" before she continued her statement, Jen planted another soft kiss on the back of her neck.

"It's okay, baby. I understand. That's what this trip is meant to do. To help you relax and start the healing process." A warm smile graced her round face as she gently rocked Karla from side to side, comforting her as the two of them enjoyed the view.

Karla did not have to tell her, she could feel her emotions. The connection that they shared was so strong that she could sense when Karla was sad, lonely, happy, and thankful without Karla even uttering a word. It seemed like when they were together, everything felt better, all the stresses of the world did not matter.

Jen also had deep-rooted issues that she was dealing with, trying hard to cope with her issues while being supportive of her lover and best friend Karla. Ever since her parents' divorce, she just did not seem to trust anyone else but Karla. Her parents had been so close;

they had seemed like the ideal couple, an established businessman with his beautiful young wife. Until one day, it happened. In her heart, she never believed the rumors that her dad had a mistress and had even fathered a love child. The young woman had added her on Facebook. Although she had the same last name as Jen, it did not strike much interest in Jen. Maybe she was a distant cousin that she did not know about.

Then it happened, the message that forever changed her life:

Hi Jen,

My name is Liz, I'm sorry to do this like this, but since our dad refuses to tell you and your mother about my mom and me, here it goes.

Your dad and my mom have been having a relationship for over twenty years now. Shortly after your mom and dad were married, my mom gave birth to me. My dad comes around here every month, we live in New Jersey. Sorry to drop this bomb on you like this but. I really want to meet you and hope we can be good friends.

Jen had contemplated whether she should tell her mom about the message for over two weeks. Finally, she decided to be honest with her mother. Pulling her aside one evening, she showed her the message. Her mother was shocked and heartbroken. When her father came home that weekend, she confronted him, and they had a huge fight that ended up with her kicking him out. The weeks that followed seemed to get worse and worse, until one weekend when she came home they both sat her down and delivered the devastating news to her.

They were getting a divorce; he was going to keep their condo in New York while she would take up a job on the small island of Samir. It was from that day she grew very distasteful of men. Most of those that she had met in her lifetime were conniving low life cheaters; even her own dad had kept such a huge secret from both her and her mother. All the while Jen never forgave her dad for all the hurt that he put her and her mother through, she also did not forgive her own self. Maybe, if she had sucked it up and kept it to herself just like he had done, she would still have her mother and father living together, happily. Maybe what her mother did not know would not kill her.

"What's up? What you thinking about baby?" Karla asked with a tone of concern, almost the same way her mother would sound when she was really worried.

It was then that Jen's thoughts were cut short. She held onto Karla even tighter than before.

"I'm happy I found you, baby. And not one of those cheating men," she said, gritting her teeth together in anger.

"It's alright, I'll never hurt you like that, my love," Karla assured her upon realizing that she was probably thinking about her dad or her ex-lover Jason.

Jason too had hurt Jen by sleeping with her neighbor. Jason was her first love, her high school sweetheart, actually. Countless times growing up they had made little vows to each other, while proclaiming their undying love, until she left and went to college. When she came back, she discovered that he had cheated on her with two of her neighbors. Not one, but two. When he admitted that he had and that he wanted to end their long relationship because of his interest in another mutual friend that they had, she was destroyed, heartbroken. It was then, that she and Karla grew even closer. It seemed like their pains and trials had only made their relationship stronger.

As they stood there on the mountain top reminiscing on the painful past, the desire to comfort each other became stronger and stronger. Soon Jen's tongue was teasing the nape of Karla's neck, blowing soft kisses upon her tender flesh. Karla moaned out in ecstasy, and closing her eyes, she tilted her head backwards, allowing Jen better access to her long gorgeous neck.

"My god Karla, you are so beautiful," Jen moaned as she kissed her neck slowly and seductively.

Karla's body yearned to be satisfied and pleasured by Jen's tongue. As she continued to kiss Karla's neck, she teased her nipples through her blouse, causing Karla to let out a series of soft moans.

"Pinch them," Karla moaned, begging that Jen pinch her already hard nipples. With that, Jen pushed her hands under the white tank top that Karla had been wearing and pulled the sports bra that she had on. Rolling it upwards, allowing her breasts to become free. With a quick movement, she spun Karla around and her lips captured Karla's perky hardened nipples, sucking them hard.

Another loud moan escaped Karla's lips as Jen sucked her nipples harder and harder. Soon Jen was pulling down on the short gym shorts that Karla had on. As the shorts dropped down to her knees, Jen immediately pulled down her panties. Her clean shaven pussy looked inviting and Jen had every intention of sucking it dry.

Putting Karla to lay down on the bare earth, she parted her legs and explored the insides of her moist wet pussy with her hungry tongue. She sucked almost every inch of it from her slit to her pussy lips to her swollen clitoris, stopping only to take a breath before continuing.

Her summer vacation of abstinence was turning into a summer vacation filled with hot sex in the outdoors. As she kissed, sucked, and licked Karla's pussy she could hear the intensity of her moaning increase and get louder and louder. Jen knew that her friend was about to reach her climax. Gripping onto the top of her hip, she plunged her tongue deep down into her wet pussy, sucking it feverishly until she heard her moan out loud the way she did when she would climax. Her juices oozed out onto Jen's tongue and she licked and sucked it all off. Her tongue lingered in Karla's pussy for some time before she rolled over and they switched positions.

Karla mounted her and began caressing her body, the way she had caressed Karla's body minutes earlier. The sensations felt amazing as Karla focused her attention on her nipples first, licking and sucking them one by one before moving downwards to her wet cunt. Moaning out loud, Jen gripped the back on Karla's head firmly and pulled her in closer, causing her tongue to go deeper and deeper inside her moistness. Her tongue swept through Jen's pussy, giving it slow succulent sucks.

"Oh my god Karla," Jen moaned as she closed her eyes and threw her head back into the bare earth. Her body quivered as Karla sucked and teased her clitoris, pulling on it lightly, causing tiny spasms to rush through her body.

With a loud moan, Jen dug her fingers into the dirt, pulling out a handful of the earth as she clenched her teeth. She was at the brink of her climax. Karla sucked her clitoris even harder, her tongue making small circular motions over and around it, massaging it lightly. With a loud moan, Jen submitted to her climax and exploded her juices over Karla's tongue. Her legs jerked forward viciously as the sensation of it all gripped her body. She took a few seconds to calm down.

Karla pulled out of her pussy and planted a soft kiss on her lips. "Now I'm really starting to enjoy this summer vacation," she whispered with a wicked little smile on her face.

Jen knew exactly what she meant. This trip was turning out to be AWESOME.

6 HER PERSONAL CHEF

The lights were dim as Bella Crusoe gazed at the foyer of her three-story mansion. The house held an eerie silence, she noted as she got out of her Land Rover. The keys rattled in her hands as she climbed the steps and opened the door. The scent of Jasmine and other indistinguishable fragrances hung in the air. The sound of her six-inch heels pierced the silence as she climbed the winding staircase. She passed the guest bedroom without stopping, then thought it over and retraced her steps.

She knocked on the door, and her personal chef and boyfriend, Alan, seemed to ignore her. She knew that he was home, since it was a weekday and he needed to serve her dinner. She tried the doorknob and, to the surprise of both the occupants inside and Bella herself, it opened. She almost doubled over at the sight of Alan and a blonde-haired woman hiding under the sheets, presumably naked, staring blankly at her. A loud gasp escaped her lips.

"Alan how you could do this to me!" she cried out. Without any cause of action, Bella turned around and stalked down the stairs.

She heard the sounds of clothes being put on in a rush, Alan and his guest racing down the stairs, the door opening and closing soundlessly, and finally a car roaring down the street.

Bella sat at the long dinner table and Alan came in carrying the dinner tray. He served her and sat down quietly. They ate in silence, and when the meal was done, Bella looked up from her plate to find Alan looking at her. She cleared her throat and broke the awkward silence.

"We're over and you are fired." Bella got up and took an envelope from a small coffee table next to the doors, which opened out into the kitchen. She slid it across the table and he took the envelope knowing all too well what this meant.

"That is the balance of last month and the whole of this month's salary. I expect you to leave my house tonight." And with that, she walked out of the dining room, chin up. Within fifteen minutes, she had emptied the guest room haphazardly and thrown the contents down the stairs. Bella locked the guest room and, later, locked herself in her own bedroom. She heard Alan collect his belongings from the bottom of the staircase.

When she finally opened her door the next morning, her mind was made up. She called the local newspaper and asked them to run an advertisement saying that Bella Crusoe was seeking a personal chef and housekeeper, females only, and that they should call her for more information. She had put her number in large curlicue numbers at the bottom of the small printout ad. Her home and cell phones were both kept on to assure that she wouldn't miss a call, and she got a lot of them. She scheduled interviews for most, given their first phone call impression. All of the interviews were scheduled for the same day at different times, giving each candidate twenty minutes to wow her. Then, she would make the callbacks, within two or three days.

On Saturday morning at 8 AM sharp, the doorbell rang. Bella was just finished adjusting the hidden cameras all over the house, including some just above all the mirrors in the bathrooms. Nothing sneaky would happen under her roof again, not by her watch.

The interviews went amazing, and one candidate swept Bella completely off her feet. Her name was Mary Alice Strong. She was a brunette, thirty-eight years old, and six years older than Bella. She exuded confidence and charm and had Bella laughing throughout the entire interview. Bella promised to call her, and then the next morning she hired her. She moved in very early Monday morning. She made them both breakfast without Bella having to ask, and they ate it, chatting animatedly at the table. Bella really liked her and she was pleasant and kind. She was the perfect chef. Her food was amazing and she seemed to enjoy Bella's company. Bella left for work almost immediately afterward.

"I will have dinner ready when you get here!" Mary Alice exclaimed, and Bella nodded before rushing out. She entered her car and roared off to her office. Mary Alice began cleaning the first floor of the house and slowly moved on to the second and third. A telltale calendar on the second floor bathroom wall showed that Wednesday was Bella's birthday and Mary Alice was already thinking of a special dinner to treat her with. When it was quarter to four, the lasagna was already cooking and she sat on the couch watching TV and eating chocolate chip cookies she had found in the pantry earlier. The oven timer went off just as the front door creaked open.

"I'm home!" Bella yelled and as she walked through the front door, she dropped her keys, handbag, and heels to the floor of the foyer.

"You're just in time for dinner!" Mary Alice exclaimed and watched as Bella came in gingerly through the doors of the spacious kitchen. "How was work?"

"Tiring, I'm so hungry I could eat a horse." Bella grinned as Mary Alice met her words with a glass of red wine. She had had a horrible day at work because the company wanted to buy another company, and they kept on changing the buying and selling rates. Bella had had to negotiate, beg, and plead to get them not to keep on changing the rates. As she was telling her about her day, Mary Alice walked busily around the kitchen, making blueberry cupcakes, with chocolate icing. Before long, Mary Alice was ushering her out of the kitchen and at the head of the table in the dining room. The lasagna, piping hot and looking delicious, was laid in front of Bella and cut up just for her. Mary Alice sat on the other side of the table and began to eat. They both looked at each other and silently begged one another to say something that would break the deafening silence of the enormous household. Finally, Mary Alice looked up from her plate.

"So, what are you doing for your birthday?" she said, and Bella almost choked on the mouth-full of lasagna she had just shoved in her mouth barbarically. Bella narrowed her eyes at her chef as she contemplated the question. After a long silence, she spoke up.

"I hadn't thought about it really." Bella smiled as Mary Alice grinned showing off her dimpled cheeks.

"Last year, I went out with some of my colleagues, but we partied too much and three of them came to work high the next morning. I vowed never to go out on my birthday again." Mary Alice gave a wink as she cleared her plate. She walked slowly and deliberately to Bella's side of the table. She picked up Bella's plate and whispered in her ear.

"Well then, hope you don't stay out too late." And with that, Mary Alice walked into the kitchen and left Bella sitting at the table breathing loudly.

Bella looked at the closing kitchen door and shut her eyes.

In her head, Mary Alice untied her spotless white apron and undid the first two buttons of her yellow sundress, revealing her white, lace bra. She beckoned to Bella and she stood, coming closer until she could feel Mary Alice's breath hot on her round face. Bella's nipples got hard and sensitive as Mary Alice's soft delicate hands roamed from Bella's full pink lips, to her sharp collarbone, tracing her neck, and finally, gripping one full breast and fondling it. Bella cried out. Mary Alice's other hand moved up to fondle the other breast through her clothes. When the teasing was over, the older woman spread her over the dinner table and parted her legs.

"Oh god," Bella moaned breathlessly as Mary Alice's tongue came crashing down on her sweet pussy.

"You like that?"

"Yes, yes, yes," Bella cried out, parting her legs further.

The feel of Mary Alice's tongue darting inside the slit of her pussy was too good to be true. Bella could feel tiny spasms shoot through her body, as Mary Alice took hold of her clit and sucked it feverishly. Her fingers soon followed suit, as she used them to explore the insides of Bella's pussy.

Sensations gripped her body and she threw her head back letting out a series of loud moans. Mary Alice was relentless in her sucking, and the more she licked and teased Bella's pussy, the closer Bella got to her amazing climax. She'd never imagined that she could have had such fun with a woman. Such pleasure. As her desire to release intensified, Bella began heaving her pussy up to meet Mary Alice wicked tongue. Over and over, she penetrated the insides of Bella's pussy with her tongue. Finally, with a loud moan, Bella summited her climax, coating Mary Alice's tongue with her juices.

Suddenly, Bella's head jerked from the dining room table. She looked at her watch and realized with a start that it was already 6 AM. She had slept at the table, and Mary Alice had not woken her up for work yet. She then remembered that she had gotten two days off because of her birthday. A small peek into the guest bedroom proved that Mary Alice had overslept and was now snoring softly into her pillow. Feeling good from her naughty little dream, Bella decided not to wake her.

Bella's new chef Mary Alice seemed to be a godsend. The two of them were getting along just fine.

"You really like my food?" She wanted to know. She watched as Bella smiled at her and sighed.

"Your food is so amazing that I smile when I take a bite. It's the reason why I couldn't wait to get home from work yesterday. Why I said I was hungry as soon as I walked through the door. It is just so amazing." Bella laughed, thinking about the ridiculous speech she had just made. Mary Alice blinked. Once. Twice. Then, she burst into a flurry of giggles. She and Bella then began to laugh so loudly that they both clutched their stomachs. After Bella joined in, they were doubling over all the way to the kitchen.

They started an accidental water fight while washing the dishes and took turns blow-drying one another's hair. Mary Alice gave Bella a massage and she gave Mary Alice a manicure, and they laughed and talked for the whole night. It was the best pre-birthday present anyone had ever given her. Bella fell asleep, feeling contented that her day had gone a lot better than expected. Mary Alice had been the most amazing company and she was so interesting. She still hadn't planned anything special for her birthday, she remembered just before dozing off. But that could be left for the morning.

Mary Alice smiled as she climbed into the comfortable bed in the guest bedroom. She had had a day that was a lot better than amazing. She felt like she had made a connection with Bella, and they had actually built a relationship that wasn't just employee-employer. They were becoming friends. And it felt...nice. She thought about Bella a lot more than often. She thought about the smooth skin that lay underneath the lilac towel that she wore today. She had changed eventually, but she had to fight every muscle in her body, to prevent herself from peeling the towel off and kissing her with a passion that she had never felt for anyone else. Her eyes began to close and she saw Bella walking toward her, slowly and seductively. Her chestnut brown eyes were closed as she came toward Mary Alice and pulled her toward her. Bella smiled and pulled her black jeans off, revealing the thin frilly underwear she was wearing. The baby blue tee came off and the bra slid off almost magically. Bella came closer and was soon stripped too. The two naked hot bodies came together. Mary Alice's hand roamed all over Bella's body and soon they both were moaning loudly.

The next morning seemed to come too soon for both Bella and Mary Alice. They both had very sexual dreams of one another the night before and they both bumped into one another when coming down the stairs.

"Hi!" Bella exclaimed and Mary Alice grinned at her. The thoughts of her fingers circling one nipple until it puckered up under her touch seemed to put Mary Alice at a loss for words.

"Um…Hi, nice to see that you're awake. I'll get breakfast started." Mary Alice continued down the stairs and finally she smiled, mostly because she had already planned to make an extra-special breakfast for Bella's birthday. So when she laid the plate with the pancake that said HAPPY BIRTHDAY in blue berries and the very special Mango juice that Bella loved more than anything else in the world and sang "Happy Birthday" to Bella, in the freaky high-pitched voice that made them both laugh when she was done, Mary Alice couldn't help but grin. And laugh and smile. They talked, laughed, and smiled the whole day, while they went shopping, holding hands in Soho, and buying the best of all outfits. Bella had the best birthday of her life, and when they stumbled back into the mansion, Mary Alice started up the special dinner and brought out the cheesecake that she had spent most of last night baking. Bella grinned and cut it more than willingly.

The conversation was kept casual, talking about the shopping trip and other miscellaneous things. Mary Alice chatted about her family, and their French ancestors, and Bella didn't hesitate to let out that her grandmother was a poor Spanish woman who made a name for herself by getting an education, which no other Spanish woman had dared to do. She went to college in America and learned how to speak English so fluently that when she had Bella's mother Annabelle, she (Annabelle) was fluent in both Spanish and English.

Bella and Mary Alice spoke and spoke until the timer went off indicating that the "special dinner" Mary Alice had prepared was finally ready. The dinner turned out to be better than amazing and Mary Alice had prepared roasted and spiced chicken thighs with a side of pasta and white wine. They ate and afterward Mary Alice escorted Bella to the roof where there was fried ice cream. They sat on a blanket, watching the stars and talking when suddenly Mary Alice turned to Bella.

"Happy Birthday..." She said and leaned in closer. Bella's breath caught as their lips met. She leaned in closer and lifted Bella's dress. Bella stood slowing slipping out of her panties. She stepped out of them and watched Mary Alice undress. Soon their bodies met and it was just as heavenly as they both had anticipated.

Their kiss was heavenly. Hungry and full of passion. Bella purred as Mary Alice's tongue explored the insides of her mouth. As they kissed, Mary Alice's hands gradually fell from Bella's thin back to her butt and she squeezed her cheeks. Bella gasped and moved her own hands to Mary Alice's face. She then slowly moved it to trace her neck and collarbone and settled on Mary Alice's breast.

She licked her finger and circled it slowly over one nipple and then the other. The nipple puckered up at Bella's touch and she smiled. Mary Alice knelt down and pulled Bella down to the blanket. There, she took in one of Bella's breasts in her mouth, pleasuring it with her tongue and teeth. Bella moaned and cried out, and that only made Mary Alice more than happy to continue.

She went lower and lower, tracing hot, wet kisses down Bella's thin tummy. Finally, she reached Bella's pussy, which was hot and wet from the enthusiastic foreplay. Without hesitation, she stuck one finger inside of Bella's pussy, causing her to cry out in pleasure.

"Oh Mary," Bella moaned out. She would now often call Mary Alice, Mary for short.

Mary continued the motion, rubbing it up

and down, and briefly pausing to lick her juices and kiss Bella fleetingly on the lips. After a while, Bella worked up some courage and slowly pulled Mary Alice up, to stick two fingers inside of her. Mary Alice, surprised at Bella's boldness, moaned in pleasure and smiled to herself.

Bella worked up her own motion, starting out slowly and getting faster and faster while Mary Alice moved her hips in time to meet Bella's long lean fingers. Mary Alice's pussy was wet, just like Bella's. They were both fully aroused and dangerously desiring to be fulfilled by each other. Bucking her pussy against Bella's fingers Mary Alice let out a series of loud pleasurable moans. It was almost as if she was in much more pleasure than Bella. Bella paused and stood up briefly. She wanted to taste Mary on her tongue, she was tired of the finger fucking, and she wanted more than that. Parting Mary Alice's leg, she slowly eased her body between the woman's inner thighs. A gasp erupted from Mary Alice's lips as Bella stuck her pink wet tongue into her slit. Licking the full length of her pussy over and over, Bella increased Mary Alice's pleasure. She served the older woman with a variety of long succulent sucks followed by quick flickering of her tongue over and around her clitoris.

"Oh god Bella," Mary Alice moaned loudly, knotting her fingers in Bella's hair and pulling her face harder against her pussy. Her actions and moaning served as encouragement for Bella, who now began fucking her pussy with her tongue, with more vigor.

"Yes, oh god, yes!" she continued to moan, closing her eyes, and licking her lips.

With a loud moan, Mary Alice summited her climax. Her juices trickled down unto Bella's hot wet tongue.

Now, it was time to get Bella to come. The two women switched positions and soon Mary Alice was pleasuring Bella more than she'd ever been pleasured in the past. Her tongue teased and massaged against Bella's clitoris. As she increased her momentum, Bella's moans became louder and more intense. With a final loud moan, she exploded unto Mary's waiting tongue. They both pulled away from each other and, with big smiles, rushed to their feet.

They picked up their clothes from the floor of the roof and carried them, naked and shivering to their separate rooms. Bella changed into a lilac summer dress with white flats, and Mary Alice changed into a blue halter dress with blue slippers. They met in the living room and the smell of fresh popcorn hung deliciously in the air. The DVD was running and the movie was on pause. Mary Alice smiled passionately and went to the kitchen to take the popcorn out of the microwave. She came back with a big bowl heaped with popcorn and small packs of heated, melted butter. They both settled into the soft couch and Mary Alice pressed play. The movie was interesting and Bella stole glances at Mary Alice while they watched.

"Enjoyed It?" Mary Alice turned to Bella when Bruce Willis turned to the detective on the screen and whispered, "Guess he had a long day." This remark made the entire team of investigators roar with laughter. Bella smiled at his bloody face now frozen on the screen, signifying the movie's end.

"It was amazing...really interesting." Bella said with as much enthusiasm as she could muster. She had barely touched the popcorn, and her soda, which Mary Alice had grabbed from the fridge, was untouched. Bella had been too busy gazing longingly at Mary Alice; she admitted to herself embarrassed. Mary Alice cocked her head to one side and squinted her eyes. Bella giggled, "You look like a confused Chihuahua!" She blurted out before she could stop herself. She let out a huge horselaugh and blinked at Bella. She smiled and brought the popcorn bowl to the kitchen, leaving her in the living room. When she returned, Mary Alice was seated on the couch, laughing like a maniac at the ridiculous actions of some random cartoon characters. The cartoon characters chased each other and one fell lifeless when the other accidentally stabbed him. He sprayed water from his nose at him and ran off. The prank left the first cat (they were cats) in a daze and soon he got up and resumed chasing the second one.

Bella laughed at the sight in front of her and Mary Alice looked at her again. She patted the seat next to her, inviting Bella to come sit next to her. She did, and soon they were both laughing like idiots at the cat and mouse's silliness. They laughed until their stomachs hurt and water flew out of Mary Alice's nose when she left the couch to get some from the kitchen. Bella caught her looking at her every once in a while, but she made sure she never caught her looking at Mary Alice. She could tell that she was completely relaxed and they had had a lot of fun together that night. They flipped through the channels and looked for something interesting to watch. They settled on a romantic movie that had started just as they turned it onto the channel. The movie seemed to be about a rich couple who was having a secret affair. Their families had forbidden them from seeing each other and they were going against each family's words.

"How romantic!" Mary Alice exclaimed and looked at Bella with her sad eyes. Bella smiled at her and she turned back to the movie. We seemed to be smiling a lot, Bella said to her and stole another glance at Mary Alice. Tears had welled up in her eyes as the girl's family threatened to have the boy beheaded.

The girl bent down on her knees pleading with her father. His stone-cold glare frightened her. The boy though, seemed courageous.

"I Love Isabel, and if I have to die to be with her in heaven, then I would do so, gladly." He said and Isabel's father tightened his hold on her. The knife burned in his hand, and if it had not been for his crying daughter, he would have pierced it through the boy's heart years ago. The girl saw her father visibly tense and at that moment, she threw herself roughly on the ground. "Father! I beg of you, do not kill him! If you do..." She added quietly, "I will take my own life to be with him in the afterlife."

Bella gazed at the TV wondering if Mary

Alice would ever take her own life for someone else. Bella looked again at Mary Alice and found that she was already looking at her.

"I would do that for you any day." She smiled and Bella knew she meant it. Bella smiled back and wondered if she meant it. She felt all squishy inside, thinking that she did. She wished that she would come closer again. Mostly so that she could try going in for a kiss. They watched the rest of the movie, and she finally yawned just as the first name went up the screen.

"I think I'm actually tired." Mary Alice said as she looked up from the TV. She looked into Bella's eyes for a very long time and soon she looked away, yawning again.

Bella could tell she wasn't sleepy, but out of courtesy, she shut off the TV and walked with Bella up the stairs. She walked her all the way to my bedroom and just as she was entering, she stopped her.

"I had the most amazing time tonight." She smiled as she blushed. She smiled as she kissed her, deeply, on the lips. She briefly said goodnight, and Bella shut the door.

7 CEO FOR LUNCH

Ashley Porter walked into the tall building nervously. It was her first day at her new job, and she looked stunning in her red business suit and blonde hair tied back into a tight bun. Her green-grey eyes were fierce, and her red lipstick matched her suit. She walked up to the front desk, and before she could open her mouth, the woman behind the receptionist booth asked,

"Good morning ma'am, how may I help?" She wore a warm, welcoming smile, so being good-natured Ashley could not help but smile back, brightly.

"I'm here to see Ms. Laura Lee Fox," she said hesitating slightly, but the woman continued to smile and glanced down at her appointment book. She looked back up at Ashley and gestured towards the elevators.

"Oh, Ms. Potter? She's expecting you. Third floor," the receptionist said. The place held a friendly aura, and Ashley was extremely enthusiastic about working there.

"Thanks," she said and moved gracefully to the elevators. When the doors closed, Ashley turned to look disapprovingly at her reflection. "I should have worn my blue suit today." She muttered to herself, and turned as the door of the elevators opened with a ding. When she stepped out, she was surprised to find herself in a magnificent office, with a plush red carpet, and a huge mahogany desk at a far corner. There was a luxurious leather couch to one end and a small chair behind the desk. In that chair was the most beautiful woman she had ever seen. She had blue eyes, which held a professional look, but was also soft; she had pink lipstick and a pink suit, much like Ashley's.

"Hello Ashley, I've been expecting you," Laura Lee said. She sprung to her feet and came around the table in a few graceful strides. "It's nice to meet such an intelligent, enthusiastic person as yourself. Your mother must be extremely proud." She said it in a manner that was so businesslike that Ashley couldn't wait to get started.

"Yes, she is. So what do I have to do?" She asked and Laura Lee smiled widely.

"Your enthusiasm is great Ashley. Well you can start off by looking at these catalogues and ordering furniture for your new office. Then, we can go to lunch." Laura Lee smiled and Ashley's eyes opened wide in surprise.

"I get my own office?" She asked and Laura Lee nodded. Ashley could not believe it! Her first day was turning out to be better than ever expected. She took the catalogue eagerly and sat comfortably in the leather couch. Laura Lee took her seat and began writing. Ashley went through the catalogue, circling the furniture that interested she, when she was done it was around 1:30 and Laura Lee was no longer in the room. Ashley got up and went to the water cooler, taking in the full majesty and beauty of the room.

"Enjoying yourself?" Laura Lee asked looking at her from the elevators. Ashley looked embarrassed because she had been caught looking around the office inquisitively.

"Um... I'm really sorry, I was just getting some water, and I was looking around, I got caught up in the—" Ashley was getting hysterical and Laura Lee could see that.

"It's okay Ashley, really, I understand," Laura Lee said, interrupting Ashley. She smiled at the younger woman as she moved back to her table. "Did you finish with the catalogue?

"Yes I did, it's right there," Ashley nodded and carried the catalogue to Laura Lee's desk. She smiled and went back to the couch, while Laura Lee made the calls to order the things that Ashley had picked.

When Laura Lee hung up the phone, she turned to Ashley.

"Do you want to have lunch?" She asked and Ashley nodded. They both got up and walked to the elevators together. When the doors closed, Ashley began humming quietly, unaware that Laura Lee was watching her intently. The elevator doors opened again, and the serene reception booth came into view.

Laura Lee walked ahead and spoke briefly to the receptionist.

"I didn't get a chance to introduce myself earlier, I'm Mary Bell." The receptionist held out her hand and Ashley took it gingerly.

"I'm Ashley. It's really nice to meet you Mary Bell," Ashley nodded and followed Laura Lee through the double doors and out into the sunshine.

"Where's your car?" Laura Lee asked and Ashley frowned slightly. There was not another car parked outside apart from Laura Lee's blue BMW and Mary Bell's pink convertible.

"I don't own one," she said shaking her head. Laura Lee was glad to give her a ride to the restaurant that Mary Bell had recommended.

"Well then hop in," she exclaimed and unlocked it. They both got in and she started the car. They chatted animatedly as Laura Lee drove through the streets of Manhattan. When they arrived at the restaurant, Laura Lee parked and they got out.

They got seats near the window and chatted until the waiter came to take their orders. Laura Lee smiled and ordered a small meal and a drink. Ashley ordered the same.

"Thank you," Laura Lee murmured as the waitress took the menus and went off. They continued talking about the new office and the job. Then Laura Lee sprang an unexpected question on Ashley.

"So tell me more about yourself," Laura Lee said. Ashley looked down at the table. Before she had a chance to say anything, Laura Lee quickly intervened.

"It's okay if you don't want to answer," Laura Lee said and smiled. She completely understood her body language, but soon Ashley began feeling bad that she didn't offer any information. So when the waiter brought their food, before they had a chance to dig in, Ashley said,

"I grew up with my mom and two brothers after my dad died when I was 10. It was pretty tough for the three of us, because my mom was really busy at the hospital, she was a cardiothoracic surgeon. My brothers eventually grew up and went their separate ways," Ashley smiled at the sad expression on Laura Lee's face. "But in case you didn't notice, I'm not exactly too comfortable with talking about my life."

"It's okay, not everyone has this luxurious life," Laura Lee smiled. Suddenly, Ashley felt curious about her boss's life.

"So what about you? What's your story?" Ashley asked. Laura Lee took a quick look around the restaurant. There was no one eavesdropping, so she took a deep breath.

"Well there's nothing much to tell. I grew up a rich girl in a rich world. My parents were these supportive people, who watched over me and took amazing care of me. When I decided to go to law school, my dad was really happy, because he was already a lawyer. My mom wanted me to be a professional designer. They both were supportive though, and I went to law school," Laura Lee smiled and took a large gulp of her soda. Ashley looked at her drinking and smiled to herself.

"So what happened after law school?" Ashley asked and Laura Lee continued as if she was in a trance, nibbling food as she went along.

"After Berkley, I worked at Angela and Associates, as a corporate attorney. But I wanted more, you know?" She took Ashley's nodding and continued. "So I started my own company, and grew it into an empire. Now see... you can work at Fox and Associates," she looked thoughtful and then looked up at Ashley again. "You didn't meet the gang did you?" And she smiled when Ashley shook her head.

They finished off their food and Laura Lee paid while Ashley waited outside.

"You ready to go see your new office?" Laura Lee asked as she unlocked the sedan. Ashley climbed in and before Laura Lee started it up, she turned towards Ashley.

"Ashley, I think you are the most amazing person for the job as corporate assistant, and I think you would do even better if you were my personal assistant," Laura Lee smiled at Ashley and she gave a little happy dance. It was obvious that she was happy about her promotion. When they stopped at the front of the office and Laura Lee parked, she turned again towards Ashley. And without hesitation, she leaned in and kissed Ashley right on the lips. Ashley's body immediately jerked back and she looked into Laura Lee's blue eyes.

"We can't do this, you're my boss," she exclaimed and Laura Lee smiled in acceptance. Ashley looked at her feeling conflicted. So with a little hesitation, she leaned in slowly and kissed Laura Lee. She was enjoying it, and her hands moved slowly up and down Laura Lee's leg. She had never seen or experienced what she was feeling and what they were doing felt so right. Involuntarily, Ashley's hand moved up to unbutton the first three buttons of Laura Lee's pink blouse. Her hand slipped into Laura Lee's shirt and she fondled one breast. The other lay on Laura Lee's thigh, where it had been from the beginning. Laura Lee gasped shortly when Ashley's hand found her breast, and her kisses got a lot more urgent and intense. Soon, Ashley began to feel uncomfortable with what they were doing and she pushed Laura Lee away.

"Morality got the best of you?" Laura Lee asked jokingly, and got serious when she saw that Ashley was frowning. Ashley was not proud of what they were doing, and she was perplexed that Laura Lee was so chilled about it. Soon enough, Mary Bell came out of the building and eyed the Sedan. She came over waving like a maniac, and Laura Lee rolled down the window halfway.

"The board called a meeting for four, you have to be there," Mary Bell said smiling and nodding at Ashley. Ashley nodded back at her.

"Hello again Mary Bell," Ashley said and smiled shyly. She could feel her face going up in flames because of what she and Laura Lee were doing just before Mary Bell came over.

Mary Bell obviously didn't notice because she looked back at Laura Lee when she cleared her throat.

"Um... Mary Bell, Ashley's going to be my new personal assistant," Mary Bell smiled at Ashley and then turned to Laura Lee with a confused look.

"But I thought she would be corporate assistant, what happened to that?" Mary Bell questioned, still confused. Laura Lee looked calm as she spoke up again.

"Well I've decided that she would do better as my personal assistant, and someone else could come in as corporate assistant," Laura Lee explained and got out of the car. Mary Bell looked dumfounded as Ashley got out and they both walked into the building. When they entered through the door, the reception room was a lot busier. Dudes in uniform walked up and down, carrying boxes and appliances.

"Is it always this busy?" Ashley asked, and Mary Bell who had just come through the doors was happy to explain.

"It's all for your new office," Mary Bell smiled and went back behind her desk while Laura Lee and Ashley took the elevator. Laura Lee punched in both the third and fourth floors this time, and got off at the third. With a parting peck on the lip, she whispered,

"Hope you like it." And walked off. The elevator doors closed then. The elevator moved up to the fourth floor, and when the doors opened, Ashley saw all the furniture she had picked from the catalogue, come to life. It was beautiful. White plush sofas lay on the white rug. Her desk was in the far end of the floor, and was white, with a white chair behind it, just like Laura Lee's. A woman stood next to the desk on the phone. She had on a white pants suit, and Ashley could see that she was not exactly a nice person. Ashley's red suit was the only splash of color in the room and as she looked around, the woman stopped talking and stared at her.

"Who are you?" She barked at Ashley. Ashley felt herself blushing again and cleared her throat a couple of times before she could summon the courage to answer her.

"Um... my name is Ashley Porter, I think this is supposed to be my office," she started and she startled Ashley by looking down sullenly at her clipboard. But her face came back up with a huge smile.

"Hello, I'm really sorry, I didn't realize. My name is Lea," she said and held out her hand to Ashley. "Well this is your office; I took care of the arrangement and placement. How does it look?" She asked and Ashley made a point of looking all around before answering.

"It's beyond amazing!" She exclaimed and Lea looked extremely pleased. She smiled and escorted Lea to the elevator. "It really is great. Thank you so much for all of this." Ashley was in a hurry to get started so as soon as the elevator doors closed, she called the third floor. Laura Lee answered on the second ring.

"Fox Associates, this is Ms. Fox," Laura Lee said and Ashley burst out laughing at the professionalism in her voice. Laura Lee seemed confused and frustrated when Ashley spoke.

"Hi Laura Lee, I was wondering what my

budget was for my office?" She asked and Laura Lee didn't hesitate.

"Three thousand, the cost of furniture excluded. Why?"

"Cause I need a laptop, and some lamps."

"Well you have it, just order it, and pick it up on your own. The company will pay," Laura Lee smiled to herself as she hung up.

Ashley made a stop at the nearest Tech Depot the next day as she walked the two blocks from her loft to the Law Firm. She ordered the laptop, and a few white desk lamps, and told them where to deliver it, and where the invoice needed to go. When she got to the building, it was peaceful. Mary Bell wasn't at her desk yet, so she just wandered through. When she entered the elevator, there was a man coming out. He had tears streaming down his face as he juggled a briefcase in one hand and his cell phone with a stack of papers in the other. When Ashley saw him, her heart melted, and she took the stack of papers from him and headed to the lobby.

"What's wrong?" She asked and he sniffed before answering. She smiled and took his hand as he set down his briefcase and sat in one of the couches.

"It's my son. He died a few weeks ago, and we, as in my wife and me, were supposed to review his will yesterday. We did, and now the lawyer is telling us that the D.A marked the will as tampered with and fraudulent. My son owned a lot, and they just discarded the will like nothing." He broke down into tears again and Ashley couldn't help but frown and she rubbed his back. She could offer him no help, she was only an assistant. So the only thing left to do was to go to her office.

"Excuse me," she muttered abruptly and hurried through the elevator door. She punched the button for the fourth floor, and as she got there, her phone was ringing. She hurried to answer it and found that it was Laura Lee.

"Hello honey, I need the criminal record of Sealy Campbell by 9 please," she said and hung up. She must be very busy, Ashley thought, and hurried out to the police archives. When she got there, the police let her in and she found the records. She hurried back to the office and stopped at the third floor. She rushed into her office and was excited to see her laptop and desk lamps waiting. Mary Bell had signed for them and she opened the first box to find her sleek, new, white Dell laptop. She opened the second box to find two white desk lamps. She had worn her all white pants suit today, and her hair formed a frame of neat curls around her head, so she looked like an angel in heaven. She placed the laptop down on the desk, positioned her desk lamps, and sat down staring at everything. She had gotten her dream job and she had never been happier.

Ashley sat at her desk when Mary Bell rang to say that Laura Lee was coming up. The elevator doors dinged and opened. Laura Lee stood like a queen, and when she stepped out, her eyes opened wide. The all-white office came as an obvious shock to her.

"It looks like heaven!" Laura Lee exclaimed and begun squealing like a teenager. Ashley couldn't help but squeal to, and soon Mary Bell came in and was overcome by the enthusiasm, so they all stood like a band of children, freaking out over their office. Eventually, Ashley and Laura Lee calmed down, and Mary Bell was soon to follow. They sat at the sofa and talked about work, and their lives. Soon Ashley, Laura Lee and Mary Bell decided to have a girl's night out, three weeks from Saturday. Mary Bell passed on her message to Laura Lee and went down the elevator. Ashley sat at her desk and typed up an opening statement for Laura Lee while she looked around her beautiful office.

"It's amazing isn't it?" Ashley asked and Laura Lee looked up. She had been gazing out of the window for quite some time, thinking about her feelings for Ashley. She was the most beautiful person Laura Lee had ever met. Ashley was the type of girl you don't say no to when she starts kissing you. She was a beautiful, strong, independent, superwoman, and Laura Lee was certain that she, Laura Lee, was in love with her.

When she had seen Ashley that first day, she had been knocked off her feet and couldn't think straight. Ashley was like a female Adonis. And now that they were in the same room, Laura Lee felt like she couldn't breathe again. It happened every single time she was around Ashley. Laura Lee smiled as she turned around to find herself face to face with Ashley. Ashley's face leaned into Laura Lee's and the world dissolved as their lips intertwined. They stood near the open window kissing, and soon, Laura Lee gently removed her suit jacket and removed Ashley's also. Ashley kissed back with an intensity and passion that Laura Lee welcomed and enjoyed thoroughly.

Ashley smiled, and continued kissing her, lifting Laura Lee's skirt slightly as she did so. She pushed the fabric of Laura Lee's panties aside and stuck two fingers inside her again; Laura Lee moaned and gripped Ashley's arms. Laura Lee's pussy was already wet, and Ashley felt elated to be causing Laura Lee so much pleasure. Soon, Laura Lee felt like she should return Ashley's favor and slowly dropped down onto the white carpet. When Ashley was firmly on the carpet, Laura Lee went down, taking one full breast into her mouth hungrily. Ashley moaned and Laura Lee moved on to the next one. She tugged and teased Ashley's nipples until they were both puckered up. Laura Lee moved lower, kissing her stomach as she went along.

When she got to Ashley's pussy, her tongue dove in, Ashley seemed to gasp, moan, and shudder all at the same time, when she felt Laura Lee's hot tongue exploring her clit, letting all her juices flow. Laura Lee seemed to make the whole world disappear as she came up slowly and kissed Ashley on the lips.

Ashley was speechless, but before either of them had a chance to speak, Mary Bell's intercom beeped, and she said that a client was coming up to see Laura Lee. This little bit of news had them both scrambling to their feet and grabbing their clothes. By the time the elevator doors opened with a ding, they were all dressed and ready to meet the client. When the man stepped out of the elevator, Ashley recognized him as the man from downstairs.

"Hi, you left so abruptly that I didn't get your name," he said and stepped into the office. Laura Lee smiled as she ushered him to the white couch. He sat and stared at the two women. "This office is beautiful!" He exclaimed and his gaze dropped to a dull white patch on the carpet. Ashley knew that that must have been where her juices were falling, so she stepped onto the patch.

"So what seems to be the problem Harvey?" Laura Lee asked and Harvey took a deep breath. Laura Lee looked at Ashley in despair, as if knowing that when Harvey sighed, there was a story to tell.

"Well I went to the D.A's office, and he confirmed what you said, so I took it upon myself to inspect the will and I found that it was completely fir…" Harvey's voice droned on and Ashley blocked it out. She thought about the intimacy between her and Laura Lee.

Soon it was time for Harvey to go. Laura Lee had given him enough legal advice and he soon left, leaving the two of them alone. Ashley couldn't handle everything she was feeling, so she calmly asked Laura Lee to leave. Laura Lee looked at her, frowning slightly.

"Didn't you want to finish what we started?" Laura Lee asked. She clearly didn't understand that what they were doing was wrong. Laura Lee was her boss, and she was a woman. God frowned greatly on girl on girl action. No matter how right it felt.

"I'm really sorry Laura Lee, but this is wrong. You're my boss!" She exclaimed before she could stop herself. Laura Lee frowned deeply now, seeing the confusion and sadness on Ashley's face.

"It's okay Ashley, I know how you feel. But I also wanted to invite you to a dinner tonight. Dress classy, and be prepared for a great surprise."

"I love surprises!" Ashley nodded her approval and walked Laura Lee to the elevator. She gave her a parting smile as the elevator doors closed. Ashley leaned against them and slid down, just thinking of Laura Lee. She went about her work with the secret love affair on her mind. She shred confidential files, ran background checks on clients, drafted two correspondences, and then she was ready to go home. She stopped on Laura Lee's floor, but she had already gone home for the afternoon. Ashley also stopped at Mary Bell's booth.

"Hey Ashley!" Mary exclaimed when Ashley stopped at the booth. "Going home for the night?" She asked smiling. Mary had seen Ashley with a glow, and she wondered what the reason was. But she knew not to pry.

"Actually, I was wondering if you knew any good boutiques which were still open," Ashley asked and Mary immediately wrote down a number of names, along with the addresses. Ashley knew she wouldn't need so many; she just needed one dress. She took the paper and stalked out of the building.

All of the stores were great, but she still hadn't found that amazing dress. It was only the one before the last that she walked into and she had found it almost immediately.

"Hi! Can I see that one over there?" She asked the saleswoman and she hurried to grab it for Ashley to try it out. It fit perfectly and Ashley bought it immediately. She went home to change into it, and do her hair and makeup in the measly one hour and thirty minutes she had left.

Ashley walked from the loft to the restaurant, and when she got there, Laura Lee was already seated and when she saw Ashley, she smiled widely. They met at the table and ordered immediately, chatting about Harvey's case. Halfway into the meal, Laura Lee mentioned Ashley's surprise again.

"So are you excited?"

"About what, you still haven't told me about the surprise," Ashley challenged, causing Laura Lee to leave the table and walk out of the restaurant. Ashley apologized, but the waitress told her that the bill was taken care of in advance. Ashley smiled and followed Laura Lee outside. There, she saw the sleek black Audi. She laughed when she saw the way Laura Lee was leaning on it.

"Is it yours?" Ashley asked out of curiosity and was genuinely surprised when Laura Lee shook her head, making her blonde hair shake and get all messed up.

"No honey, it's yours." Laura Lee smiled and Ashley squealed with delight. She had gotten her driver's license a few weeks ago and was about to buy a car, but Laura Lee solved all her problems. She ran across the narrow street, to Laura Lee. Just to give her an earth-shattering, toe-curling kiss. They stood there in the street, arms around each other, as Ashley smiled when she thought about the perks of being in love with the boss. And boy, were there perks.

8 A MARDIS GRAS AFFAIR

Tina watched as her best friend Joanne continued packing her bags in anticipation of her trip to New Orleans. For weeks now, Joanne had been begging her to go to the Madri Gras festival in New Orleans. Joanne was overly excited about the entire thing, and Tina just could not understand the reason for all the excitement on Joanne's part.

"It's a silly festival, where all kinds of stuff happens, and I'm not talking about good stuff, Joanne," Tina made one final attempt to change her friend's mind or even caution her perhaps.

Joanne turned her head slightly, placing the article of clothing that she held in the bag before responding. The look on her face was clearly that of an irritated young woman. "Why you always gotta be like that, Tina? Just because you don't like it doesn't mean it's bad.

Okay?"

Tina threw her hands up in the air in frustration; she just could not get through to her friend. "Fine, Joanne. I won't say anything else about it. Go ahead!" with that she left their small dorm room and headed to the cafeteria for dinner all alone.

Normally the two of them were inseparable; they had breakfast, lunch, and dinner at the café together. Added to that, they ensured that they did most of their college classes together. Their friendship had seemed very solid until now. But now Tina was seeing a side of Joanne that she had never seen before—a wild side, carefree and not bothered by any of Tina's warnings.

Joanne had always been the quiet, more submissive one of the two of them. The fact that she was now very feisty and persistent about going to the Mardi Gras parade was a shocker for Tina. Although she hated admitting it, Tina was somewhat turned on by the sudden change in her best friend's personality.

For some time now, Tina had been developing an attraction for the calm-natured Joanne. The fact that they shared the same quaint little dorm room did not help the situation either. Uncertain as to how Joanne would react if she made any advances, Tina kept quiet and continued to secretly lust after her best friend.

As she sat at the cafeteria table having dinner alone, a feeling of loneliness and despair crept upon her. Tina wondered whether she had been too hard on the girl whom she had shared many happy times with in the past three years of college. It was seldom that Joanne ever showed such zeal and desire to go somewhere and partake in something. Most of her time was spent in her room studying, and when she was out, she was either in class or at the laundromat doing their laundry. Tina hated doing laundry and was quite happy when Joanne offered to do hers in exchange for her taking out their trash.

Tina chuckled at the thought of their little arrangement. They almost seemed like a married couple where the husband and wife shared their chores. She continued to take huge bites of the roast turkey on her plate.

"So you didn't even wait for me, ma'am?" the question came almost suddenly. Tina looked up to see the faint smile on Joanne's face. Thankfully, she was good-natured and rarely took anything to heart. Tina's storming out on her back at the dorm was actually a little funny to her. Tina was acting like a spoiled brat, as usual, and Joanne found humor in the situation.

"You didn't want to listen to anything I had to say. So I left," Tina pouted her lip with her statement. Looking up at Joanne, she realized that there was not a sign of a frown on her face. "Come join me?" Tina was determined to now put their little argument behind her. Maybe going to New Orleans would have been fun. Just what she needed after her rocky start in this new spring semester.

"So how much is the ticket?" Tina asked her friend.

"Oh goodie, you thinking about joining me, aren't you?" Joanne knew Tina all too well. She wouldn't be asking about the cost of the ticket if she was not interested in taking the trip with her.

"Not much, I'll be taking the bus. It'll be like the college road trip we never had," she laughed, nudging Tina at the same time.

"Figures please…?" Tina gave her a stern look. Joanne was evading her question. She was considering going on the condition that the ticket was fewer than one hundred dollars. And even then, she'd be dipping into her little piggy bank to come up with the money.

"If you want to go, I'll pay."

"Oh no, I wouldn't ask you to do that Joanne."

"It's not a problem Tina. Just say the word and we can go online to purchase the ticket now. I have the extra money from my refund, and I've been saving it for something like this," she gave a little chuckle while Tina maintained a straight face.

"Come on. Please come," she coaxed, as she leaned in and grabbed Tina's fork, taking a bite of her food.

Tina and her friend spoke for almost an hour. The entire time Joanne was trying to convince her that taking the trip to New Orleans could be a fun and exciting opportunity. A once in a lifetime trip, she had said before they ended their conversation. By the end of dinner, Tina had made up her mind; she was definitely going to take the bus down to the Mardi Gras festival in New Orleans with her best friend Joanne. As they sat in the computer lab, Joanne assured her one more time that everything was going to be okay. With that, she put in her credit card information in the required fields on the purchase form and clicked the "Order" button. Her transaction went through and she printed out the receipt for the bus ticket for Tina.

"So we're doing this for real, Joanne," Tina said, giving her friend a warm smile. Excitement slowly consumed her and she longed to be at the much talked about event.

The four-hour bus ride was finally over, and as they disembarked the Greyhound bus, Joanne flipped open her cell phone and called someone. It was her cousin Ashley who lived a short distance from the bus station.

"Okay, no problem, we'll be there," Joanne said as she ended the call with her cousin. Joanne seemed to have family in every state or city. As soon as she arrived in New Orleans as expected, she had a family member that she called, a distant cousin by the name of Ashley.

Joanne informed Tina that she had arranged for them to stay with Ashley for the duration of their stay. They walked over to the fast food restaurant that Ashley had asked them to meet her in; it was only about half a mile away from the bus station where they had arrived.

In the next few hours, they'd be going to the Mardi Gras parade. Soon they met Ashley and she drove them over to her house. Along the way the girls were fascinated with the beautiful decorations that hung everywhere along the streets. And oh, the people—most of them—had masks on their faces and colorful beads draped around their necks. They all seemed to be having fun and enjoying themselves.

"Wow, I can't wait to join in," Tina cooed with excitement in her eyes.

"Well I never thought I would hear this coming from your mouth," Joanne chuckled, quite amazed at her friend's statement. Not too long ago, Tina wanted nothing to do with the idea of traveling to New Orleans for Mardi Gras, yet here she was right now, excited and highly anticipating the event.

"I don't know. I think it has something to do with the atmosphere; most people can't resist the urge to join in," Ashley added, with a smile on her f ace. She knew all too well how people could easily change their mind about the event when they got to the venue.

It took those about two hours to get dressed before heading out to the streets to be part of the festive celebrations. Tina wore a pair of short denim shorts with a blue tank top, while Joanne wore black shorts with a pink tube top.

As they joined the people celebrating in the streets, soon they were having the best time they had ever had in their entire life. Several glasses of red wine along the way made the experience all the more exciting. Finally, after hours of celebrating going into the early morning, the three young women headed back to the house where they intended to spend the night.

Joanne and Tina shared a small bed in the guest room of Ashley's two-bedroom house. As they laid there in the bed, the alcohol seemed to begin to set in. Tina slowly brought her lips to meet Joanne's, kissing her passionately. Their kissing was titillating and full of passion. Joanne moaned as she locked lips with her friend, her hands roaming freely all over Tina's body.

"Oh Tina, I want you so much," she cooed, bringing her lips down to Tina's neck, sucking on her tender flesh.

"I want you too Joanne," she moaned, tilting her head back and exposing her neck father for Tina's caresses.

They slowly and quietly undressed each other; they were extra careful. They didn't want to wake up Ashley, who was sleeping peacefully in the room next door. Tina had the perkiest breasts Joanne had ever seen, and she thoroughly enjoying sucking on them. Her tongue caressed each nipple with care and precision while her finger stroked her moist heat.

Spreading her legs further, Joanne indulged on Tina's temple of delight, working her tongue from her anus all the way up to her swollen bud. Tina cooed as Joanne's tongue pleasured her more than she'd ever been pleasured in her entire life. Bucking her pussy against Joanne's mouth, Tina rotated her hips, heaving her pussy slightly off the bed. Joanna sucked her pussy feverishly, darting her tongue into Tina's core, pushing her closer and closer to the brink of her orgasm.

Finally, with a loud moan, Tina exploded, coating Joanne's tongue with her sweet juices. Satisfied that her friend was fully pleasured, Joanne switched places with Tina. It was her turn to be on the receiving end of Tina's tongue.

"Oh..." she cooed, as Tina plunged her tongue deep into her temple of delight. Her body shook viciously from the intensity of the moment as Tina darted her tongue in and out the slit of her pussy. Working her way up to Joanne's clitoris, Tina sucked hard, licking it all over.

Joanne couldn't control herself; she let out a series of soft moans that had Tina soon covering her mouth to muffle her cries.

"Carefully baby, we don't want to wake your cousin up," she gave her a little smile before retreating to what she'd been doing. It felt good to taste her best friend, and to see her struggle to maintain control felt all the more better. It was like a dream come true for both of the young women. For some time now, they'd both been harboring their feelings for each other, each one too afraid to make the first move. Finally, with this trip to New Orleans, they had gotten the opportunity to do something wild and erotic in the spirit of Mardi Gras.

Joanne tasted just as she'd imaged, sweet and delicious, and her moaning seemed to be from deep down within. It was like taking a trip on the wild side. Joanne had always been very quiet and settled, and to see her come out of her shell and let it all out was quite thrilling for Tina. These thoughts motivated Tina to suck harder—she wanted to see her friend basking in the ecstasy of the moment.

Fully motivated, she began sucking harder, making pleasurable sounds as she went along. Finally, with a low, stretched out moan, Joanne reached her climax, her body quivering from the pleasure of it all.

It took them both a few minutes to calm down. They were without a doubt tired and spent from their moment of ecstasy. Quietly, they changed into their pajamas and then returned back to the bed. Within a few minutes they were both lost in a deep sleep. Visions of their time together consumed their dreams, and as they held onto to each other, their dreams became sweeter and sweeter.

Morning came almost too soon, and as the two friends woke up, images of a wonderful night flashed through their minds. If anyone had told them that they would have had such a great time, they would have called it a bluff.

"So I was thinking, maybe we can rent out a small motel room or something," Joanne suggested. Although it was okay staying with her cousin, the fact that they weren't alone was somewhat of an obstacle. She wanted to be able to fully enjoy Tina's body without the fear of her cousin hearing or, even worse, walking in on the two of them. They needed privacy. And a motel room could offer the type of privacy that she wanted to have with her friend.

Tina didn't hesitate at the idea either. She too was somewhat uncomfortable, having sex at a stranger's house.

"The entire time, last night, I kept thinking—what if Ashley wakes up," she admitted.

"I know, that's why I was extra quiet too. I felt like I would die at one point. I wanted to just scream out with pleasure, but I couldn't because I didn't want to wake her up," Joanne added.

Upon reaching their decision, they informed Ashley. Thanking her for her hospitality and a good time at the parade, they made their way out of her house. They had told her they were returning home, and when she offered to drop them back off at the bus station, they informed her that there was no need as they'd be getting a ride with a friend.

When the taxicab came to pick them up from her house, Ashley gave them curious looks, but they assured her that they were just going to meet their friend, saying that the taxi was just a little more convenient than having her drive all the way to Ashley's house. They would meet up with her in the city and then she'd drop them off.

"Well okay. If you guys want to do all that, then I guess it's all up to you two," she had said with a confused look on her face.

"Yes, we don't mind at all; you've been more than kind to us, and we couldn't ask you for anything else," Joanne gave her a warm smile as they left her house and walked to the cab that was outside waiting.

The motel was about twenty minutes away, and when they got there, it was partly empty. A young man stood at the front desk and welcomed them with a faint smile on his face. He seemed pretty frustrated with his job.

"Here's your key, and if you need anything you can dial zero for the operator," he said in a mechanical-type voice.

He seemed so unenthusiastic about his job that it was almost as though he didn't want to be there. Maybe he'd been at the parade last night and was tired and spent from all the festive activities of the night.

Anyways the two friends decided to ignore the receptionist and made their way up the stairs to room number twenty-three, where they would be spending the night.

The room was small, almost like their dorm room, with the exception of the fact that it had a little kitchenette in it and their own private bathroom. Back at the college, the dorm rooms had shared bathrooms between them. And so two rooms shared one bathroom, and four people were forced to use the same bathroom.

"Well at least we have our privacy," Joanne chuckled, realizing the disappointed look on Tina's face.

"At $49.95 a night, what did you expect Tina?"

"I know...I know...I guess, like you said, the good thing is that we have some privacy...And now, I can really do and say what I want," she grinned, a little devious look swept across her features as she took slow steady steps towards Joanne.

"Okay, hold on. We have the entire night for ourselves. First, we need to get some stuff for tonight," Joanne informed her, pulling her small brown wallet out of her duffle bag.

"Stuff like what?" Tina asked curiously. She was there on this trip, almost penniless. The thought of having to buy stuff was scary considering the fact that she had less than ten dollars in her wallet.

Joanne must have realized the worried look on her face, and she assured her that she would not have to spend a penny. "I was thinking of getting us some strawberries and chocolate syrup, a bottle of wine too, perhaps."

"Really, that sounds...that sounds like a great idea," Tina admitted hesitantly. It was not that she wouldn't enjoy all these things; it was just that she knew that she had no money and Joanne had already paid for everything so far, and she didn't want her running out of money trying to impress her. After all, this little detour at the motel was a new expense that they had not budgeted for.

"Well if you have the money, then let's do it," she finally said, not wanting to disappoint her friend. Joanne's eyes lit up. She was so excited that she almost jumped for joy.

They left the motel briefly and walked down to a small grocery store about ten minutes away. There they bought strawberries and chocolate syrup. They picked up the red wine at a liquor store a few blocks down from the grocery store.

When they got back to the hotel, they were hot and sticky and so they took their showers separately. Tina was the last to get out of the shower, and surprisingly, as she made her way out, she caught sight of Joanne on the bed naked with strawberries spread out all over her body. She looked like a model right out of a magazine—the type of models that would lay naked with their privates covered in fruit or raised petals.

"Whoa! you look amazing."

"Thank you, sweetheart," Joanne cooed, parting her legs open, exposing her bare pussy for Tina.

Tina slowly dropped her towel to the floor, revealing her naked body. Swinging her hips from left to right, she walked over to the bed, where Joanne laid waiting.

"I really enjoy your company, Tina," Joanne stated, closing eyes and dropping her head down onto the bed. She lay back looking up at the ceiling as she spoke.

"I love your company too; you're a really nice person, Joanne. How exactly do you not have a girlfriend?" Tina asked. Although they were best friends, she couldn't help but realize that Joanne didn't have a boyfriend or a girlfriend. Joanne sighed deeply, contemplating the question. Finally, she turned towards Tina. She wore a warm smile, and Tina felt the intensity of her gaze as she spoke. Her voice was low and quiet.

"Well, I've never found a girl that I really like," she answered, resisting the urge to add, "except you." She closed one eye. Tina assumed it was all too painful for her to admit and that she was trying to convince herself to open up further about her love life.

"What's wrong with me, Tina? Why can't I find someone special?" she sobbed suddenly. Joanne was an average college girl with black hair and deep blue eyes.

"Maybe, that special someone has been there all along. Maybe you just didn't know it was..." She stopped for a minute, trying to gather her thoughts. "...It was you," she added, with a smile on her face.

Tina turned towards her and, without thinking, took her into her arms. She didn't resist, she wanted Tina just as much, and she'd actually fantasized about Tina for a while now. Joanne kissed her, first just a small peck on the lips and then a passionate one that lasted a lot longer. She moved her hands up and down Tina's spine. Joanne subtly moved her hands down Tina's body and gripped her butt. Squeezing her butt tightly, Tina squealed in pleasure. Tina's hands also roamed all over Joanne's body, finding her huge, melon-shaped breasts and kneading them with her hands, pinching their perky nipples occasionally. Tina sucked in a huge breath when Joanne's lips left hers and took in her nipple. Her tongue moved viciously over the right nipple while her fingers fondled the left. Finally, she released her nipples and pulled away briefly.

"Thank you so much for coming here with me. You've made me one of the happiest people alive. Who would have thought that Mardi Gras would have turned out so great?" Joanne admitted, reaching over to the bottle of red wine, which had been on the nightstand. She poured them both some red wine in the plastic cups that had been in the room. Next, she took the chocolate syrup and spread it all over Tina's body, dipping the strawberries that had rolled off her body onto the bed, into the syrup.

Bringing the strawberry up to Tina's mouth, she invited her to indulge in the sweetness. Tina did not resist, she took a slow succulent bite of the chocolate-covered strawberry, closing her eyes as she chewed. They continued eating the strawberries and chocolate syrup with the red wine. They were in no rush; they had the entire night to themselves. This was years of pent up desires, and they had every intention to take things nice and slow.

"I brought a strap-on," Joanna informed her.

Tina nearly spurted out the wine she had in her mouth from the shock of Joanne's statement.

"A strap-on... I didn't even know you had one of those," she said with a curious look on her face.

"There are still so many things about me you don't know, sweetheart," Joanne teased, reaching over to her duffle bag in the corner and pulling out the strap-on penis. She attached it to her waist area and returned to the bed to meet her friend.

She sat down and captured Tina's lips with hers, kissing her passionately while slowly lowering her onto the bed. Her hands roamed Tina's body while her tongue explored Tina's mouth. Her lips moved downwards to Tina's breasts that were fully exposed. Joanne took in one breast, pleasuring it until she moaned. She then moved on to the next one and grazed it gently with her teeth. Tina's nipple puckered up in response and Joanne smiled, sucking on it harder; she sucked so hard that after a while Tina was literally crying out. Joanne then moved lower down and unbuttoned her blue skirt.

Finally, she released her from nipples and penetrated her moist pussy with the artificial strap-on penis. At first, her thrusts were slow and steady, but as the intensity of the moment grew, so did the momentum of Joanne's thrusts. Soon she was making Tina's entire body shudder. The room was filled with their moaning and panting. Over and over, she penetrated her temple of delight until she let out a loud moan and her juices spurted out of her. Realizing that Tina had just reached her amazing climax, Joanne lowered her lips to meet Tina's and planted a soft kiss on them.

"Did you enjoy that?" Joanne asked curiously. Tina nodded, obviously at a loss for words. Her eyes were closed and she did not see when Joanne took off the strap-on.

"Here, your turn." Joanne rolled over and laid on her back, parting her legs open in anticipation of Tina.

Tina slipped it on and entered her, slowly at first, but she soon picked up the pace, ramming the penis into Joanne's wet pussy.

"Oh God, yes! Don't stop, Lord, My goodness!" She exclaimed, her voice filled with desire. Over and over, Tina thrust the penis into her pussy, groaning and making pleasurable noises as she went along. Finally, with a hard thrust, Joanne gripped her ass tightly and let out a loud scream of pleasure. She had just reached her climax. Her juices coated the artificial penis.

Tina collapsed onto the bed, tired and spent from it all. They had just had an experience that they would never forget—an unforgettable erotic experience while at Mardi Gras.

9 A DAY IN THE LIFE OF A PORN STAR

"Jump in, Lisa!" Macy exclaimed as she stopped right in front of me with her brand new red Mustang convertible.

"I'm so jealous, girl!" I said as I lamented the fact that we both finished high school together, we both couldn't afford college, and yet she could afford to have her heart's desire while I, on the other hand, had to work my butt off to survive.

Macy and I had been friends for a while now, but lately I had noticed that life had become easy for her - very, very easy. I so wanted to get in on whatever she had been up to, but I felt shy asking. I was never one to pry into anyone else's business, regardless of the fact that we'd been good friends for years now.

Tonight we had decided to go see the latest vampire movie that was out in cinemas everywhere. We raced down the avenue since we were late for the 7 o'clock movie. It had been forever since our last girls' night. I missed those days.

Sadly, we got to the movies late and weren't able to get in to see the vampire movie. But there was another good movie playing. It was a paranormal movie. Not exactly my favorite pick, but it would do.

The movie went well and, for some reason, the screening room we were in was quite full. Screams could be heard every time there was a really scary scene. It was as if we were actually living the movie. I enjoyed every bit of it.

"I'm so not gonna get any sleep tonight," said Macy as she held on tightly to my arm. I agreed with her, as this had been one of the most thrilling and frightful movies I had seen in a while. I could feel every strand of hair on my skin standing erect, even after it was over.

Before heading home, we stopped off at the Yum Yum Better Ice Cream store because I had to have my favorite birthday cake ice cream. There, we sat and spoke. Sitting across from Macy, I couldn't help but notice her expensive diamond earrings, which beautifully complimented her emerald-colored Versace tube dress that clung perfectly to her fair, smooth skin. And how could I not notice her Christian Louboutin sandals? Without a doubt, she was the hottest girl I knew, and I although she was my good friend, I was secretly beginning to envy her a little.

I finally developed the courage to ask about her job, or whatever it was that she did with her time. Clearly, it was bringing in a lot of money. After all, no one could afford these expensive articles of clothing and jewelry without having a great source of revenue.

"So Macy, I've been thinking," I started. "You're my girl, right?" I wanted to establish the fact that we were good friends, and good friends, in my opinion, help each other out.

"Yeah, what's up?" she replied, eager to hear what was next. "I've been noticing you rocking the latest styles of everything, and I was wondering if you could hook me up." Her face lit up with a guilty smile as she responded. "If I told you, I'd have to kill you, girl."

I cringed a little. Was she into something illegal? I should have backed down at that moment, but I was persistent. I needed to know what it was she did. I asked again, desperate to be in on her little secret. She hesitated before she finally opened up slowly.

Once we got deeper into the conversation, Macy explained that her new job was a secret but was nothing that she couldn't introduce me to, given that I had an open mind. I had always been the quiet reserved type of girl. Even my mother had a tough time with me growing up and socializing. While my older sister would be out with her friends, taking trips to new places, and meeting new guys, I would stay indoors engrossed in my novels. It was time that I did something different. Something that was new to me and that, in the end, would make me happy. I needed some excitement in my life.

Macy too had always tried to get me out of this shell of mine. She assured me that her job would be perfect for me. Not only was it interactive but it mixed the right amount of business with pleasure.

"Pleasure," I sighed as I thought about it. Ever since my break up with Tommy I hadn't been satisfied sexually, except for my one-on-one scenes with myself, when my body and mind couldn't overcome the urges that plagued me, especially in the late hours of the night.

"Please, Macy..." I cooed, giving her a desperate little look. I was almost like a child at the candy store, begging for some candy.

"Alright, alright. I'll see what I can do, but don't judge me, okay?" she replied.

So Macy called up her boss that same night. Surprisingly, he seemed eager about having a new team member. Although she still didn't let me know the details of the day ahead, she suggested that I wear something sexy, revealing, with some stilettos, red perhaps.

"Put some curls in your hair, and put a light shade of lipstick on. Don't wear too much makeup though. We'll take care of all that. Just ensure that you look your best. It's going to be intense over there. I just want you to be able to fit in as best as you can." She had a serious look on her face as she spoke.

A nervous feeling swept through my body. Whatever she was into must have been pretty serious. Was she into dealing drugs? No—she couldn't be. I knew her, and she was not that type of person. She didn't even drink or smoke, much less do drugs or try to get others to do them.

What job did Macy have, and why did I have to dress sexy for it. Was she a stripper? I laughed at the thought. No—not my Macy. No way, she didn't seem like to type to get on a pole in front of several men. Nope, she couldn't be a stripper.

After being dropped off home, excited about the next day, I searched my wardrobe for my sexy red skin-tight dress. Thoughts ran through my mind all night long. I tried to imagine a list of jobs that she could possibly be doing. Finally, I gave up at about midnight. "Time for bed, stop thinking about it," I coached myself, shutting my eyes for the night. While lying in my bed, I came to the conclusion that whatever it was that Macy did for a living, it was bringing in a substantial amount of money. And she seemed happy, very happy, spoiling herself with luxurious gifts. I wanted that too, and tomorrow would be the day when I would make my life-changing decision. If she was rolling in the dough, I was ready to join in. Upon making the decision to proceed with whatever offer her boss made me on tomorrow, I smiled and drifted off into a deep sleep.

"Beep Beep Beep," the sound rang through my room. My eyes popped open as I jumped out of sleep, awakened by the alarm clock that sat on my nightstand. "Ah...shit...7:20," I muttered to myself, realizing that if I didn't get off my bed in the next few seconds, I could possibly end up being late. I turned off the mechanical device angrily and closed my eyes. Thoughts of last night's erotic dreams crossed my mind. My heart was racing, and it was still skipping a beat every now and then. My nipples were pinched stiff as I rubbed my fingers lightly over them.

I remember being in a room where the lights were dim and red. It had high walls, and the room was not so wide. Looking around, I saw two females, both wearing masks that covered almost every part of their round faces, except their piercing blue and green eyes. They were both wearing knee-high leather boots, and one wore black leather stringed underwear, while the other was topless. As I searched deeper in my mind to relive my dream, it became more and more vivid. I was lying on a lounge chair in the room, and the two girls came closer and sat next to me.

The first one with the blue eyes began kissing my neck while the other one pushed her hand under my skirt. Her hand met the cloth of my underwear and she slid it down slowly. I gasped when her hand slid into my slit and pleasured me. Her fingers were long and firm, and as the first girl moved lower to my breasts, I let out a long moan, laced with the sound of pleasure.

"You're so sweet," the first girl whispered, bringing her fingers into her lips and tasting my juices.

The other girl nodded, taking her turn, as she slipped her index finger into my pussy and licked it as well.

"So, so sweet," she whispered to her friend.

They helped me relax on to the lounge chair, parting my legs open. A wave of pleasure shot through my body as the second girl plunged her tongue deep into the slit of my pussy, flicking it vigorously inside my core.

I let out a series of soft moans, each one growing a little louder than the last. My fingers knotted her hair as I pulled her face harder against my pussy. I wanted more; she seemed to be an expert at what she was doing.

While the second woman hovered over me, she took one of my perky nipples into her mouth. As she sucked on the right nipple, her hand fondled the other. Taking the left nipple between her thumb and forefinger, she rubbed it lightly, tugging on it occasionally. I let out several little moans of pleasure.

The more they pleasured me, the closer I came to my amazing climax. I begged the woman who had her face buried in my pussy to suck harder. She happily obliged, sucking more feverishly and gently tugging on my clitoris as she went along. I closed my eyes, bucking my pussy against her face. She continued sucking while the other woman continued caressing my nipples. With a loud moan, I reached my climax and coated her tongue with my juices.

The sound of the phone ringing pulled me out of my thoughts.

"Hey Lisa, you up?" Macy's voice sounded on the other end of the line.

"Yeah...I'm about to hit the shower," I informed her.

"Oh ok, well, hurry up, you don't wanna be late. Jerry doesn't like tardies...Anyways I'll be there in the next fifteen minutes...Don't keep me waiting," her voice grew stern towards the end.

Macy knew a lot about me, and the fact that I was usually late for everything seemed to worry her, especially this morning. She was my reference, and if she brought in someone who didn't seem to be able to pull their weight, she'd end up looking bad in the end.

"Enough lazing around," I told myself. It was time to get out of bed.

The sun was just rising as I stumbled out of bed and rushed to the bathroom. The face that stared back at me looked refreshed and alive. I felt well rested and ready to take on Macy's challenge. I showered and put on short red dress that I had been saving for a special day. It hugged my figure perfectly. A deep V cut was in the front, exposing the top part of my breasts. I'd always been told, by both women and men, that I have beautiful cleavage. And today seemed like the excellent opportunity to flaunt it. I wore a pair of red stilettos that coordinated with my dress. With one final look in the mirror, I took a long, deep breath and then walked out of my apartment. I looked fresh, and even felt fresh, when I stepped into Macy's car.

"Look at you!" She exclaimed. "Love the outfit, good choice," she added, and we drove off. We didn't speak on the way, and she soon stopped at the gates of a huge mansion. The intercom beeped and she said her name. With another beep, the gates opened and she drove through and up the long driveway. When we got out of the car, Macy walked quickly to the door and knocked on it five times, leaving a two-second pause between the second and fourth knocks. The door opened slowly and when we both walked inside.

I gasped in amazement. "What's going on here?" I asked Macy, who had a little smile on her face. There were naked women everywhere. They walked around, comfortable in their own skin.

"Come in over here, you'll need to see Jerry and speak with him for a few minutes," Macy said as she led me to a small office in the back.

As we walked to the office, she disclosed her secret to me. She worked in adult entertainment, as a creative director. "So basically, you're into making porn?" I had a shocked look on my face. Never did I imagine that this would be her job.

"Well...I'm not exactly in the videos, I just basically direct them. Tell the girls what to do and stuff, that's pretty much it. You know me, I could never just get up in front of people and show off my body...naked," she gave a little chuckle after she spoke.

To me, it sounded pretty much like the same thing, whether you were in the movies, or directing them. Porn was porn. There was no way of sugar coating it. "Creative director, ha," I thought to myself, amused at how she had disguised what she really did.

Jerry was her manager. He signed off on

everything that was recorded. Today, she'd introduce me to him. He had liked her, and from day one, she'd been promoted to a director. She'd never had to act in any of the adult movies. And my, was she happy about that.

Tapping on the door lightly, she waited for Jerry to answer.

"Who is it?" a husky male voice called out from behind the door.

"It's me, Jerry, I've got Lisa here with me," she replied.

"Come in," his voice softened up.

I was shocked to see Jerry in person. I had imagined him to be a perverted looking older man. But, surprisingly, he was a handsome fellow. He had light blue eyes and deep brown hair. He smiled as Macy introduced me to him.

"Hi, nice to meet you," he replied when I told him my name. He was dressed well, in a black suit, and he looked incredibly handsome at his huge mahogany desk.

"Well, before we do anything, here's the non-disclosure agreement, that needs to be signed. Take a minute go through it and then we'll take it from there," he handed me a thick pile of papers with about ten or twelve pages.

I sat in the chair before the desk while Macy excused herself, leaving me alone with her boss to go over the rules and regulations. I browsed through all the pages before finally signing and dating the agreement page, which happened to be the last page in the set of documents.

I handed him back the agreement, and he

went through it, briefly emphasizing what I had just read.

"Miss Carter, you understand that this non-disclosure agreement that you've just signed is between you and Sweeter Girls Galore Incorporated. You must not tell anyone what you have seen or participated in today. You also understand that all sexual acts performed here can and will be posted on our website, www.sweetgirlsgalore.com. You also confirm that you are above the age of eighteen and that you are willing and consenting to the list of activities listed on page 6, in our clause agreement."

"Yes," I replied with a little smile on my face.

"Okay great, just needed to go over that. There will be security around at all times, and you'll be required to take an STD and HIV test before we begin. Do you have any questions?" He lowered his gaze to meet mine, as if trying to tell me to ask him something—anything.

"Well, do your online movies ever get put on DVDs and resold?" I inquired. My opinion was that the Internet was huge, and the chances that someone I knew would stumble upon one of the movies that I was featured in were slim. However, if they were put on DVDs, then that could mean they might be available at local video stores, and that's something I didn't really want to happen.

"Don't worry, we are strictly online, we don't ever put our stuff on DVD. And if, per chance, we did, we'd let you know in advance." He smiled a warm sincere smile.

"So today, I have you for a college sex

scene. Basically, the set will be in a dorm room, and then you'll be banging your roommate," he chuckled, his eyes lighting up as he laughed.

"Yeah, that sounds good," I assured him.

"Okay, let me get Macy back in here to show you around," with that he picked up his phone, made a quick call, and in a few minutes my friend Macy was back in his office.

"She's good to go," he grinned a devious little grin.

"Great," Macy indicated that I follow her. She took prompt steps that had me believe she was in a hurry.

Turning around suddenly, she looked at me and said, "I know you're nervous, but it'll be okay, I promise. I wouldn't let anything happen to you anyways," she smiled.

We got to large room that appeared to be a college dorm room. There were two small twin beds lined next to each other. One wall had the poster of the actors in the latest vampire movie. A small computer desk and chair were tucked away in a corner. The scene almost brought me back to my college days.

Macy walked me through everything: how I should act and what I should say. It seemed pretty easy, but the nervous feeling that I felt was almost unbearable. Why did it seem so easy for her, yet so difficult for me?

"Take a deep breath," she urged, before

stepping back and having a little chat with one of the camera guys. She returned and walked me to the bed, coaching me once more before they began filming.

"I get it," I assured her with a long sigh.

"Okay, well, here we go. Just act normal and I think you'll really enjoy the whole experience."

She left briefly and stood next to the cameraman at the main camera, situated to the front of the room. There were cameras everywhere, shooting from almost every angle.

I sat on the bed with my reading glasses on. I had a book in my hand and I was pretending to read. I had the role of a nerdy college girl. A few minutes later, another young woman walked in. Her name was Isabella. She had beautiful blond hair and a gorgeous figure. She wore sexy lingerie, similar to what I was wearing. We almost looked like twins, excepting the fact that we had different hair color.

We spoke for a while, as if we were two roommates, and then finally she took a seat on the bed next to me. Her lips slowly met mine as she explored the inside of my mouth, kissing me passionately.

Her tongue was hot and warm, and her hands roamed freely all over my body. She panted as she lowered me onto the bed. I helped by spreading my legs open as she began slowly caressing my body with her tongue.

"Oh baby," I moaned out, licking my lips and smiling at her. I'd been told that I had to occasionally lick my lips and smile. And so I did just that.

"You've been a bad, bad girl," Isabella whispered, pulling off my bra, exposing my gorgeous full breasts.

I could see the look of lust in her eyes. She was turned on instantly by my breasts, and I could tell. Taking one into her mouth, she sucked long and hard on my nipples.

"Oh yeah, baby," I moaned again, this time closing my eyes.

"I'm going to suck that little pussy dry. You hear me? Dry." She used her hand and smacked my pussy lightly through my lace thong.

"Ah...god...yeah," I cooed, licking my lips again and taking a long, deep breath.

Isabella released my nipples and used her tongue to trace downwards, all the way to the center of my womanhood.

I let out a loud moan as she captured my clitoris with her mouth, sucking on it feverishly, while her fingers stroked my moist tender flesh. I wanted more, and so I asked.

"Fuck it, baby," I begged. "Please?"

She spread my legs further. "POV, Allen," I heard Macy order from the corner where she was now standing. With that, one of the camera men walked up closer to us, focusing the lens of the camera on my inner thigh and what Isabella was doing down there.

Isabella adjusted herself to where the camera had a clear view of her tongue stroking my pussy lips. I moaned out, forgetting everything and everyone around me. The feel of her tongue on my pussy was driving me near the point of insanity.

I raked her hair with my fingers, pulling her harder against my pussy. My toes curled up involuntarily as I struggled to maintain control of my body. Waves of pleasure coursed through me as my juices flowed freely out of my pussy and onto her waiting tongue.

She continued increasing my pleasure by darting her tongue into the slit of my pussy over and over.

"Oh dear mother of god!" I moaned breathlessly, bucking my pussy against her lips. Sensations griped my body as she tongue-fucked my pussy.

With a loud moan, I exploded onto her tongue.

"Switch," I heard Macy's voice instruct, and Isabella stood up slowly and stretched out her hand to meet me.

"Now it's your turn, baby," she whispered, her eyes lighting up.

"AND ACTION!" Macy instructed.

I lowered her onto the bed and, using my mouth, I pulled her panties down. I then popped her bra open. She let out a light moan, her voice laced with anticipation.

I quickly began fondling her breasts, licking and sucking them, pleasuring her just as she had pleasured me. Isabella moaned out, begging me for more. Using my finger, I found her moist heat and worked my way inside her, thrusting my fingers into her slit several times.

I pulled my fingers out of her pussy and sucked the juices, "Delicious," I cooed, returning my fingers to her wet pussy.

10 SEDUCING LA MAESTRA

I stood in the doorway of my dorm at Grambling State University. I looked down at my friend Steven as he tied his shoelaces. He looked up at me as if I was crazy.

"Gosh... Ms. Ramirez," He said for the third time. We were on our way to our academic advisor's office to get approval for the elective courses we had just picked out online. As he said her name, flashes of the sexy calculus teacher flashed through my mind. I held my class schedule in my hand. It showed that the sexy Ms. Ramirez was going to be my calculus teacher. I couldn't wait for my first class with this gorgeous, seemingly young lecturer. Ironically, I had never been so excited about calculus.

"Yes! She's so hot!" I cried as Steven locked the dorm door. He gave me a curious look. He must have been wondering why I would be interested in a female lecturer. After all, I was a female myself. My sexual preference for women was something that I never shared with him. We started walking and I decided to change the focus of our conversation to his attraction to her.

"You know that she's a professor, right? And that she would never give a student like you the time of day?" I teased winking at him.

"Pessimist," he shot back, throwing me a dirty look. He sighed and then stopped at the door of the administration building. I stepped ahead of him, noticing the womanly shaped shadow forming behind the glass door.

"Excuse me," I said smoothly, stepping aside allowing the middle-aged woman to walk past me.

"Hi Logan," her voice was low and calm. I stood still, dumbfounded. How did she know my name? I gave her a faint smile while curiosity swept across my face.

"How do you know my name?"

"Doesn't everyone know you?" she whispered and walked off. I looked at her over my shoulder until she seemed to disappear in the sunset.

She was a gorgeous woman. Her high cheekbones and dimpled chin made her all the more stunning. She wore a professional looking black suit with a pair of black stilettos. She was the type of woman that I hoped I could be one day: a beautiful, career-driven woman.

That night when I got back to my dorm room, thoughts of Ms. Ramirez plagued my mind. She even consumed my dreams. I had images of her spread out on a desk with her pussy bare, begging me to taste it.

When I woke up, I was starving. I stumbled through the dorm, tripping over textbooks and my laptop charger. As I opened the small door of the mini fridge, I realized that all I had in there was... ice. "Shit, I'm out," I muttered to myself. Today would be one of those days where I'd have to get something to eat from the college cafeteria. I hated going to the cafeteria for one main reason—the huge crowd of students and teachers that assembled there. Arriving there, I noticed a familiar person eating a small sandwich. I quickly paid for my slice of cheesecake and made my way to the person's table.

"Hello, Logan," she said before I could even address her. She looked up at me and gestured at a seat I could take. With our first class being in a few minutes, I thought that this would be the ideal opportunity to get to know her outside of class. I smiled at her and took the seat she pointed to.

"Hello, Ms. Ramirez." I gazed longingly at her as she took another bite and tentatively wiped her mouth. She looked up at me; her eyes held a mischievous glare. As she smiled, we began talking. We spoke about a series of topics. She told me about her jobs before she came to Grambling, and soon, after I started talking about my parents, she also started opening up.

"I grew up in San Francisco with my mother. She was a corporate lawyer. My dad died when I was seven." She said, and she closed her eyes. "My mom married a senior lawyer from another firm, and they didn't pay that much attention to me." She looked at me and I beamed at her. She smiled widely in response and looked astonished when I blushed. I waved my hand signaling that she could go on. "My mom made sure that I went to school, and I could basically do whatever I wanted afterward. She made enough money to ensure that I was fully taken care of. I did whatever I wanted on the weekends and my mom could not care less. I left high school, I asked for my trust fund, and I left for Ruston. So, what about you?" She asked and smiled at me. I cleared my throat.

"Both my parents died in an accident when I was three and I was adopted by new parents. My mom was a real estate agent and my dad was an engineer. I grew up in the best elementary, middle, and high schools, and was privately tutored for three months before applying to Grambling." I looked at her and was a little surprised to see tears in her eyes. I smiled. "What's wrong?" I asked, fighting the urge to kiss her passionately on the lips and tell her that everything was going to be alright. She looked at me and smiled sadly.

"Nothing," She whispered, wiping her tears in a way that wouldn't ruin her mascara. She looked at me and turned around in her seat. She was obviously looking around to see who might have seen our slightly emotional exchange. Satisfied that no one was around, she finished off her sandwich and wiped her mouth. She then got up from the table abruptly and glanced at the confused look on my face.

As time went by, Ms. Ramirez and I became closer and closer. It was Saturday and she had invited me to come over to her house, to help with preparations for a small party she was having. Sadly, by the time I did my laundry and cleaned my room, it was rather late. I called her to inform her that I would be arriving late. But she didn't seem to mind at all.

The party went well, and since I'd missed the preparation part, I decided to stay back and help Ms. Ramirez, or Maria, as she asked me to call her. Everyone had already left when it happened. We were saying goodbye to each other when she leaned in and gave me a soft peck on the lip. I didn't resist her. Her actions served as fuel in a fire that I had been secretly concealing. I immediately pulled her in and captured her lips with mine.

Her lips were soft and tender, and on her breath, I could taste the wine that she had been drinking. I wanted her, and by the way she was animatedly kissing me, I knew that she wanted me back. As we continued kissing, I could feel the saturation in my panties. My hands soon travelled along the length of her body.

"You have gorgeous breasts," I blurted out, massaging her melon-shaped globes through her white cotton dress.

"Thank you," she cooed, giving me a sheepish smile. Her lips found mine yet again.

As she explored the insides of my mouth, I wanted nothing more than to take her back inside and love her the way only a young college girl could.

Her lips left mine and dropped down to the nape of my neck. I let out a soft moan, realizing that she had just turned the tables on me: I was no longer in control of the situation. Pulling down on the top part of the tube dress that I had on, she released my perky, petite breasts. I had always been a slender young woman, and at twenty-three, the only thing that seemed to have blossomed a little was my breasts. They were gorgeous, hands down.

"Oh god," I moaned out breathlessly as Maria took one of my hardened nipples into her mouth. Pinning me against the wall, she sucked the nipple with so much vigor that I thought I would lose my mind. As she sucked on one nipple, the other nipple was stimulated with her thumb and her forefinger as she pinched it lightly. Sensations gripped my body as she pleasured me with her tongue. I could feel my juices trickling down my pussy and my body ached for more of her sweet caresses. Never in my wildest dreams did I ever think that this day would become a reality. I'd often dreamt of kissing Ms. Ramirez, feeling her tongue in my mouth, tasting, and feeling her lips. But never in my dreams did I think that her lips would be on my nipples, sucking them as her hands stroked the rest of my body.

When she slipped her fingers into my moist core, I gasped for air. Sliding two fingers inside my pussy, she pleasured me with her fingers. I was wet; so wet my pussy throbbed in anticipation of her fulfilling me.

Ms. Ramirez pulled away for a brief minute and led me to her couch. She invited me to have a seat while she went into the kitchen to get us something to drink. This was against my better judgment and, had I been under twenty-one, I would not have accepted her offer. She soon returned holding two wine glasses in one hand and bottle of red wine in the other.

"I've been saving this for some time now," she whispered, using her tongue to trace along my earlobe. Tiny spasms shot through my body as she helped me relax on her huge leather couch.

Parting my legs, she buried her face between my inner thighs. I let out a soft moan as her tongue made contact with my moist, tender flesh. At first, her movements were slow and succulent. She worked her tongue from the slit of my pussy all the way up to my swollen bud, taking my clit into her hungry mouth with much more urgency than I'd expected.

"Lick it," I begged, as she released my clitoris and began licking it slowly. To me, she seemed like an expert, working her tongue over and around my clit, sucking it occasionally. I could feel my juices making their way from the top of my spine to my hungry pussy.

"Ah..." I cooed as she flicked her tongue over my clit. Her fingers soon followed, stroking the walls of my pussy. She seemed to be enjoying herself just as much as I was.

"Is that how you like it?" she whispered, with a little devious smile on her face.

I nodded my head, unable to even utter a word. She intensified my pleasure when she began darting her tongue into the slit of my pussy while massaging my clitoris with her index finger. Bucking my pussy against her touch, I let out a loud moan as I summited my amazing climax.

Ms. Ramirez smiled and a look of satisfaction swept across her beautiful face. "Now let me," I urged her, indicating that I wanted to switch positions. I wanted to pleasure her the same way she had just pleasured me. She didn't have an ounce of resistance. She stood, briefly undressing before me. Her body looked amazing; I could tell from her perfect abs that she worked out quite a bit.

I parted her legs and brought my lips down to her sweet, wet pussy, licking it feverishly from her slit to her clitoris. She moaned out loud, begging me to suck it hard. I happily obliged, sucking it with much more vigor and precision. I could feel her body intensifying as my tongue swept through her moist heat. Her legs jerked viciously as her fingers dug into the leather couch. With a loud prolonged moan, she reached her own climax.

We sat on the couch for a few minutes and calmed down. A warm smile lurked on her face as she spoke to me. We discussed the current economic situation and how things had changed. I loved to watch her giggle when I would occasionally give a little joke. She would throw her head back and let out a little laugh, covering her mouth so it didn't come out too loud. Her eyes would light up as she brought her head back down, her gaze meeting mine every time.

The weeks following our little erotic experience were amazing. We would sneak into her office after class and explore each other's bodies right then and there. I think we both got a rush from the fact that we could get caught, and it made the sex all the more exciting. As the semester came to an end, so did her tenure at the college. She would be moving to take up a new job in Chicago. "Teaching is not for me anymore," I remember her saying a few weeks prior, when she gave me the news. Her new job paid double what she was currently making, and to her, it seemed like the opportunity of a lifetime. However, what was good news for her ended up being bad news for me. I would miss her terribly. At first, I tried to be happy for her, but I could not conceal my hurt and sadness for long.

As the time approached for her to leave, I finally decided to accept the future. If we were meant to be together, nothing would prevent that. Distance would be a non-factor, and our love would overcome it all.

Today was her birthday and I had every intention of making it the happiest day of her life. I had planned to cook a nice home-cooked meal. Her favorite dish actually, sausage and pepper lasagna. She had given me the keys to her house so that I could begin making preparations there. After all, I was still a college student living in a dorm room that had just a few appliances, and an oven was not included.

I got there early and immediately started gathering my ingredients. Her fridge was loaded with groceries. It was almost like being in a grocery store. "My gosh," I thought to myself, "Does she ever cook." Everything was neatly organized and seemed untouched, to say the least. It didn't even appear as though the house was occupied.

Later on in the evening, Ms. Ramirez arrived home looking tired and spent.

"Happy Birthday!" I rushed over to greet her at the door.

"Thank you," she smiled, giving me a warm, loving look.

In her hands she had a plastic bag with the name "Anna's Fun Stop" written across it. Anna's Fun Stop was the name of an erotic store across town. They sold stuff ranging from dildos and vibrators to some of the more complex sex equipments.

"I see you've been shopping," I teased.

"It's all for you. Funny how it's my birthday, but I'm out getting you stuff. Ahhh... well," she grinned as a devious look swept across her features.

What the hell did she mean? Like she'd said, it was not my birthday. So why she was out getting me gifts?

"Well thank you, ma'am," I leaned in, reaching for the bag in her hand.

"Not so fast, young lady," she pulled the bag away from my grasp. "The night is still young." With that, she strode past where I was standing and made her way upstairs, turning around to give a seductive look before continuing on her merry way.

I left and made my way back into the kitchen to plate our food. I had stumbled upon her wine cellar in the back and had taken the liberty of getting us a bottle of wine for dinner. I hope that she'd be okay with my little indiscretion.

I waited for her for a while before I finally heard the sound of her heels clicking on the hardwood floor. She was approaching the kitchen at a steady pace.

My jaw dropped when I saw her. She looked stunning. Her beautiful pink satin gown flowed perfectly on her body, accentuating her curves in all the right places. Her hair was loose and hung in medium-sized curls. My eyes travelled up and down her body several times, taking in her beauty. To me she was the sexiest woman alive.

"Wow, you look ah- amazing," I stammered, trying hard to get the words out. She was a breath-taking, gorgeous woman, and anyone who didn't appreciate that was a fool.

"Thank you, sweetheart," she whispered to me as she continued walking toward the dinner table where I was seated.

Throughout dinner, I couldn't stop looking at her. She would giggle when she caught me staring, saying that I was just as beautiful as she was. "How sweet of you," I would reply, convinced that she was just trying to make me feel good about myself.

Although I was not insecure about myself, I was also a very real type of person, meaning I knew there were other women, such as Ms. Ramirez, that looked twice a beautiful as I was. And I didn't mind at all, I was fully comfortable in my own body.

We ate the food and drank the wine. She said that she had absolutely no problem with me going into her wine cellar. "Mi casa es su casa," she said in Spanish. I gave her a curious look, wondering what the heck she'd just said. If there was one thing I was not good at it was speaking and understanding Spanish, or any other language apart from English.

"It means my house is your house. It's what we used to say when we wanted someone to feel welcome," she chuckled at the look of confusion that lurked on my face.

"Oh," I laughed, "Well, munches gracia," I managed to say. I think that meant thank you in Spanish.

"You mean, muchas gracias," she chuckled again at my poor pronunciation.

"Yeah, I think that's what it is," I laughed.

"Sweetheart, munches and gracia, aren't Spanish words," she laughed.

We continued talking while enjoying dinner. Everything went well and, as the night progressed, I found myself highly anticipating what was to come. The one other thing that kept lingering on my mind was the fact that she'd said she bought me something special. I wondered what it was.

After dinner, Ms. Ramirez led me upstairs

to her bedroom. It was huge—double the size of my entire dorm room. A large king-sized bed covered with white satin sheets was in the center of the room. Above the bed was a huge mirror on the ceiling.

"Come over here, I've got something for you," she said, leading me over to the bed. "Close your eyes," she further instructed.

I did exactly what she had asked without an ounce of hesitation on my part. Anxiety gripped my body. What the heck was she planning to do with me? I thought to myself.

Using a blindfold, she covered my eyes while I stood next to the bed. Suddenly I felt her hot wet tongue forcing a passionate kiss upon me. Her kiss was vicious almost, full of life. As we kissed, she slowly began undressing me. Finally, she was satisfied when I was completely naked. A shiver ran through me body as I stood there, unsure as to what to do next.

Leading me to the bed, she spread my body onto the soft satin sheets.

"Oh..." I cooed, as her tongue travelled the length of my body from my long neck to the core of my womanhood and further down to my toes. Taking my toe into her mouth, she sucked it hard. This brought about a sensation I had never felt before. I moaned out as she continued to suck my toes one by one.

When she left my toes, her tongue travelled to my inner thighs. She spread my pussy with her fingers while her tongue probed the inside of my pussy, sucking all of my sweet juices while massaging my clitoris occasionally. I could feel my passion building up and her tongue seemed to devour my wet cunt.

Then, without warning, I felt it. A sudden thrashing, with a whip. I gasped as she continued flogging my pussy with a whip. Was this the gift that she was talking about? No—it couldn't be, I thought to myself. Then another strange object made contact with my temple of delight; a part of it hugged tightly onto my clitoris while the other part of it was used to penetrate my pussy. Over and over, she plunged the artificial cock into my moist heat, whispering obscenities to me as she went along.

I moaned out in ecstasy. Never in my life had I felt such an amazing device on my pussy. And trust me, I'd experimented quite a bit with a few erotic sex toys. But this one was new. She continued stimulating my clitoris while fucking my wet cunt. I wanted more and she could tell. Pulling the device away suddenly, she decided to use her fingers and her tongue instead. I always appreciated an all-natural feeling.

Her tongue stroked the tender flesh of my pussy from the bottom of my anus all the way to my swollen bud. She took my clitoris into her mouth and sucking it hard each time she got to it. She slipped two fingers into my wetness while her tongue focused on my clitoris, sucking it slowly at first, then hard and with much more vigor, as her fingers jabbed into my core over and over, relentlessly. I moaned out and several cries of pleasure filled the room. She too was enjoying it, because she was panting heavily from brining about such pleasure upon me.

Bucking my pussy against her finger, I let out a loud cry as I reached my earth-shattering climax.

I cooed as my juices coated her tongue and fingers. I took a few minutes to calm down before we exchanged positions.

"This is for you," she said, handing me a strap-on penis that she took out of the bag of sex toys she had next to the bed.

"So this is what you got me," I smiled.

"Yep, hope you enjoy using it."

"I will, but not as much as I hope you enjoy it when I am fucking you with it," I teased.

"Exactly, you see, I'm killing two birds with one stone," she chuckled, giving me a little wink.

Without further hesitation, I attached the strap-on penis to my body and mounted her. I stopped just seconds before penetrating her pussy. She gave me a curious look that seemed to shout out, "Hey, what the fuck are you doing?"

I decided that I needed to taste her pussy first. Bringing my head down to her inner thighs, I gave her a long, slow lick.

"Oh god, yeah!" she moaned breathlessly as my tongue continued to stroke her moist core. I spent a few minutes pleasuring her with my tongue, bringing her closer and closer to her climax.

Finally, I pulled my mouth away from her pussy, satisfied that I had gotten her to the point that I wanted. Without warning, I mounted her and penetrated her wet pussy with the strap-on penis. She moaned out, parting her legs even further, giving me better access into her pussy.

I began thrusting the penis into her pussy, slowly at first, then increasing my momentum as I went along. She moaned out, her cries laced with delirium. Bucking her pussy against my body, she heaved her hips to meet my thrusts. Finally, with a loud cry, she summited her climax, coating the strap on penis with her juices.

I rolled over, tired and spent from it all. She gave me a little grin of satisfaction. I didn't know how the future would be for us, but I did know that I'd just had one of the wildest experiences of my life with Ms. Ramirez.

"Hey, wake up," I could hear my friend calling in the distance. I opened my eyes. We were sitting outside the administration building.

"What are we doing here?" I asked curiously. The last thing I remembered was making love to Ms. Ramirez.

"What? We're waiting for them to approve the elective courses we just picked out, of course."

It was then I realized that I had been daydreaming about Ms. Ramirez. I took a deep breath as my academic advisor called me into her office. Hopefully, if she approved my calculus class with the woman of my dreams, Ms. Ramirez, I may just be able to make my dreams a reality.

AUTHOR'S NOTE

Readers: I want to expand a few of the stories to see where the characters can be explored further. If there are any of the stories that you would like to read more about again, I'd love to hear from you!

Visit my blog at www.shalabreece.com

Join my newsletter for free exclusive previews
http://www.shalabreece.com/in

Follow me on Twitter at
http://www.twitter.com/shalabreece

Like my page on Facebook at
http://www.facebook.com/shalabreece

Discover my books at major ebook retailers everywhere.